BIGFOOT AND THE LIBRARIAN

LINDA WINSTEAD JONES

Cover design by Elizabeth Wallace
http://designwithin.carbonmade.com/

❀ Created with Vellum

CHAPTER 1

THIS WAS *NOT* what Marnie would call a stellar beginning to her new life. Normally a flat tire wasn't a disaster, but she was smack dab in the middle of Nowhere, Alabama, parked crookedly on the grassy shoulder of a narrow tree-lined road, with zero cell service. She had maybe an hour before the sun set.

Her new job at the Mystic Springs Public Library had seemed like such a good idea when she'd set out from Birmingham. It was going to be a new beginning, perhaps even an adventure. She could use a little adventure in her dull life. She'd been happy to leave her old job and her sweet but less-than-brilliant former boyfriend behind, and had actually dreamed of the perfection that was Mystic Springs. It had to be perfect! It was a small town with a well-stocked library manned by a single librarian. That librarian was soon to be her.

Not that she'd ever actually been to Mystic Springs, knew anyone who lived there, or had ever talked to anyone who'd been there, other than the town council representative who'd offered her the job over the phone, but in theory it was the perfect solution to her current life bump-in-the-road. *In theory.*

Could taking on a small-town library really be called an adventure? Why not? Anything was possible.

Mystic Springs was located south of Eufaula, Alabama. She'd checked it out on an online map before setting out in her usually reliable — but not at all adventurous — car. The small town was bordered on the east by the Chattahoochee River, with two much narrower waterways running along the northern and southern borders. The town was nestled in the horseshoe plot of land between those three flowing bodies of water. Maybe there really was a spring somewhere, mystic or otherwise, but she hadn't seen it on a satellite image. She'd tried to zoom in, on her phone and again on her laptop, but the picture had remained annoyingly blurry.

She should've done more research on her new home, but she had not. Being laid off just a couple of months after deciding that no matter how sweet and devoted and ripped Jay was she'd never be able to teach him to pronounce the first "r" in "library" or have a meaningful conversation about anything other than his workout sessions or sex, she'd been eager to move on.

Jay — thirty years old and his mother still called him "JayJay" — would be fine. Before leaving town, Marnie had introduced him to an equally beautiful, and equally dim, woman who didn't have to worry about pronouncing "library" correctly because she'd never been in one. And never would. Not that Marnie was judgmental or anything, but still…

Getting fired was never fun, but she had to face facts. It had been time to move on.

Mystic Springs was the first stop in Marnie Somerset's well-planned new and improved life. She was twenty-eight years old. Her wild oats and romantic mistakes — *ahem*, Jay — were behind her. Only great things lay ahead. Head librarian would look great on her resume. If Mystic Springs wasn't the idyllic place she imagined it to be, it could just be the first stop in this new phase of life. She'd move to a bigger city, by thirty, she imagined, where she'd run one of the premier libraries in the country and marry Mr. Darcy. Well, someone like him. She would fall in love with a man who was cultured, civilized, and romantic, and he would fall in love with her. It wouldn't hurt at all if he looked hot in a waistcoat.

Many of her peers disdained Mr. Darcy and said his kind was out of fashion, but not Marnie. She'd always been a bit out of step, had accepted that about herself long ago. Who wanted to be like everyone else? Not her. She'd read Pride and Prejudice at an early age, and had always imagined Darcy as the perfect hero. Maybe in reality he'd need some work, but all in all… yummy.

In her mind he did look an awful lot like one of the actors who'd played him in a movie, but that was neither here nor there.

Marnie waited by her gray Nissan with the flat tire for almost forty minutes, hoping a car would drive by. She climbed into the car and sat in the driver's seat now and then, but it was stifling hot and she didn't dare keep her car running for the air conditioning. She wasn't out of gas yet, but she was running low. On occasion she stood by the hood of the car and held her cell phone high in the air, hoping for an errant bit of cell service to miraculously shine down upon her phone. Nada.

There weren't a lot of options. By the time she walked back to the highway — and appearances aside it *was* an official state highway — where she would eventually be able to flag down a car or a truck, it would be dark. She wasn't sure exactly how far it was to town proper, but it was a walk she wasn't eager to make. All she could see between her and Mystic Springs was a winding, tree-lined road. And trees. Lots and lots of trees.

She pushed her glasses up on her nose and looked down at her shoes. Any woman who was five foot two on a good day wore heels as much as possible. Not for hiking, though, not for walking down a narrow road on a warm summer night. She glanced in the direction of town. There were a lot of potholes ahead. It could be dangerous to walk along that road once it got dark. There was a flashlight on her phone, but it wasn't powerful enough to light more than a step or two ahead. That would be better than nothing, she supposed, but not by much.

It had seemed like such a good idea to ship almost all her things ahead. Sensible walking shoes — along with all her other stuff, from furniture to knick-knacks — awaited her in her new home, a small house no more than two blocks from the library. She had never imagined she'd find a job in the field she loved that came with a more than decent salary *and* a house. How lucky was that?

Efficient movers had come to her apartment on Friday and packed up almost everything she owned, and then Marnie had spent the weekend with her best friend, Chelsea. They'd eaten nachos and drunk too many margaritas and watched sappy movies on television. Chelsea had taken today off, so they could have coffee and cookies and one last hug, before Marnie headed out for her new job and her new home.

The councilwoman who had hired Marnie, Susan Tisdale, had sent a photo of the house by email. That pic had been grainy — who didn't have a decent camera on their cell phone? — and only of the charming outside. Grainy or not, the cottage looked like something out of a fairy tale, or a BBC period drama. In reality the place might need work, she really had no idea, but it would be the first time since she'd left her dad's house that her home wasn't an apartment. She wouldn't have to smell what the neighbors were having for dinner, or know precisely when the woman upstairs exercised.

Zumba.

All Marnie had with her was her purse, her laptop, and a small overnight bag with an impressively stocked cosmetics bag and a couple changes of clothes. There was one extra pair of shoes in the bag, uncomfortable but really cute sandals with kitten heels.

Why hadn't she shipped her makeup ahead and kept a pair of running shoes in the car? Not that she ever actually ran…

"I give up," she said, resorting to talking to herself. Car locked, purse strap on her shoulder and damned useless cell phone in her hand, Marnie started walking toward town. She was used to the heels, she normally wore them at work all day, but she knew it wouldn't be long before she was cursing her preferred footwear. Optimistic, she held her head high and took long strides down the deserted road. A horrible thought crossed her mind. What if she'd taken a wrong turn? What if Mystic Springs *wasn't* straight ahead? To the right, the land was undeveloped and thickly wooded. To the left, some attempt had been made to clear away the brush here and there. Still, there was no sign of life.

She'd been walking ten minutes — seemed more like thirty but the clock on the phone still worked — when she approached a turnoff on the left side of the road. Overgrown shrubs and a stand of spindly trees hid what was beyond the gravel road until she was right upon it.

Marnie stopped. Blinked. Stared. Then she sighed in dismay. The windowless building, which was about the size of an average convenience store, sported one bare lightbulb near a rusted metal door. A single — also rusted — red pickup had been parked near that door. Did someone live there? Was it a business of some kind? Maybe it was a workshop, or a warehouse. For a few seconds she considered walking to that building, whatever it might be, and knocking on the door. The rusty truck belonged to someone. That someone had to be in the creepy building.

She lifted her cell phone high and prayed for a signal. *Just one bar, please. Just one single bar.* Nothing.

From beyond the rusted building, something unseen howled. A shiver walked down Marnie's spine.

That building was not at all appealing. It didn't even look safe. The truth was, the entire area kind of gave her the willies, even without the distant howl. But she'd come this far. She could walk a while longer. She couldn't be far from town!

Not far past the creepy building stood a corroded metal sign welcoming her and anyone else who might venture down this road to Mystic Springs. It leaned crookedly to one side and was mostly covered by tall, climbing weeds. She was, so far, unimpressed. Still, the sign was a, well, sign, that she was close to her destination, that this was indeed the correct road.

She walked another five minutes, noting the encroaching darkness, looking left and right hoping for some indication of life. A subdivision that backed up to the road, just on the other side, maybe. A small business or cabin or RV tucked in the woods. There had to be someone out here! That search was as fruitful as her quest for a cell signal. Holy cow, what had she gotten herself into? Had she really been hoping for an adventure? This was definitely not what she'd had in mind.

She was not a fan of sweat, but she was sweaty now. Years ago, before she'd run off to Colorado with her old high school boyfriend, Marnie's mother had told her women didn't sweat, they glowed. That had pretty much been the extent of Carolyn Somerset's motherly advice. Marnie had never glowed so much. Her blouse stuck to her back, and a trickle of sweat ran down from her temple to her chin. Her favorite bra, the one that offered support while actually being somewhat comfortable, had moved beyond slightly sticky to damp.

Finally, she caught a hint of motion out of the corner of her eye. Just ahead, to the right, something moved. Leaves rustled. Something... breathed? Snorted? She stopped, peered into the shadowy woods for a long moment and then called out a hopeful, "Hello?" as she tried to scan the darkness beyond the road. She held her breath and listened hard for an answer. Did she want someone — or something — to answer, or not?

She was an optimist most of the time, but when there was no answer she began to wonder if maybe she shouldn't have braved the creepy building. Who — *what* — was out there? Anyone? Anything? Silly, she chided herself, working to make her heart return to a normal rhythm. The disturbance in the woods was just an animal. Nothing more. A squirrel, or maybe a raccoon. Nothing larger, she was sure of it. Birds! Yes, that was it. Birds could make a lot of noise in the brush.

Just ahead, movement again drew her attention. The leaves of a tree near the road shimmied and shook. That was *not* her imagination! It wasn't a bird in the brush, either; it was far too big. Had to be a man. She smiled, lifted her hand to wave — and dropped it again as the hairy thing stepped into the road directly ahead.

What the hell? Marnie straightened her glasses, leaned forward a little, and squinted. Whatever that thing was it was seven feet tall, hairy from head to toe, and it stopped in the middle of the road to turn and look directly at her.

She quit breathing for a long moment. If that beast rushed her, she wouldn't have a chance. Even without the heels, her legs were too short to outrun something like that. Her imagination whispered *Bigfoot*. Her logical brain whispered *no way*.

Her primitive survival instincts whispered *run*.

She did.

Clint pulled his truck into the back parking lot of Harry's, the only bar in Mystic Springs, and the only place in town to buy a hot meal after 7 pm. Monday wasn't the busiest night of the week for the bar and grill, but there were a couple of cars in the back lot. Like most of the locals, he parked in the back and entered through the unmarked side door that squealed as it swung open.

From the outside Harry's was unimpressive, to say the least. It was purposely uninviting; there wasn't even a sign indicating that it was open to the public. Beyond the door the bar-and-grill was sparkling clean, with four cushy booths, a half dozen tables, a polished wood bar, and a retro juke box. The floor was black and white tile squares; the booths were red and the tables gray. More than one neon sign lit the bar, as well as a few overhead lights that were bright, but not too bright.

He saw her right away. Who wouldn't? Strangers didn't come to Mystic Springs often. It was too far off the beaten path. And a stranger who looked like her? Never.

The brunette had thick, wavy hair, dark-rimmed glasses that complemented her pixie face, a summery blue outfit — the short skirt showed off her fine legs — and matching blue high heels. She stood in one corner of the bar with her cell phone held high.

"There!" she said, relief in her voice. "A signal! Just one bar, but..." She smiled for a moment, but too soon the smile vanished. "And it's gone."

She turned around and looked critically at the handful of men in the bar. Harry stood behind the bar, ignoring her. Jim and George — two old coots who were on those same stools six nights a week — continued with their conversation, also ignoring her. She likely wasn't accustomed to being ignored, especially by men.

Strangers weren't welcomed in Mystic Springs. Not even when they looked like this one. Strangers were definitely not welcomed at Harry Milhouse's place.

Idiots. If they helped her, she'd be on her way. The longer she was here, the more likely it was that she'd see something she shouldn't.

Her gaze continued to sweep the room and they stopped on him. Her eyes, so wonderfully dark he could tell even from here, widened. She pushed the glasses up on her nose, shifted her weight from one foot to the other, and gave him a look that was absolutely, positively pitiful.

He should follow the example of the other locals and ignore her. She was trouble; he could tell that with one glance.

He walked toward her, his steps slow and hesitant. What the hell? "You look lost. Can I help you?"

Wow. Chiseled jaw, dark blond hair, and all of six foot... three? Four? However tall he was, this guy was all muscle. In blue jeans and a button-up checkered shirt, he looked kind of like a lumberjack. As far as she knew, there weren't a lot of lumberjacks in Alabama.

Marnie took a deep breath. She did not need another good-looking, muscle-bound, sex-on-a-stick man to get under her skin. Not even for a minute. She did her best to ignore the fact that she was sweaty and flustered, tried to keep her voice cool as she answered his question. "I've had a flat tire, and I can't get enough of a cell signal to call AAA." She held the phone up, as if offering proof. "My car's just down the road, but..."

She should've walked back to the highway, she knew that now. Too late.

The three men who'd been here when she walked in had been less than happy to see her. Jerks. The interior of the rusted building was much nicer than she'd imagined it could be, but the people were not. The guy behind the bar had been pissed that she didn't want to order a drink, as though alcohol would make things better at this point. She'd asked him if he had Merlot, or any other red wine, because it did seem like she should order something. He'd laughed at her. The same way he'd laughed when she'd asked if he had a phone.

The glass of water he had grudgingly served her had been lukewarm.

"Do you have a spare?" the new, hot, lumberjacky guy asked.

Marnie nodded. "Of course. Not that I know what to do with it." She felt like such a girl. After this, she was going to learn how to change a tire! She didn't really want to have to change a tire, but it would be a skill in her toolbox. A new skill for a new life.

"I'll take care of it."

So, chivalry was not entirely dead, after all. It was just on life-support. "I hate to ask…"

"You didn't ask, I offered." He made it sound like a done deal. "Mind if I have a bite to eat first?" He headed for the bar. "I'm starving."

She would never say so, but she did mind. A little. She was so eager to get out of here and on into town! She didn't know what awaited her in Mystic Springs, but it was sure to be better than this. There had to be a shower in her new house, and goodness knows she could use one. Was that why her knight in shining plaid had offered help so quickly? Did she look that bad? She was the picture of sweat and desperation. Oh, God, she probably smelled terrible.

It would be impolite to tell him his supper had to wait, so she muttered a soft, "Sure."

Marnie wondered if she dared to tell this man, or anyone else, what she'd seen as she'd walked down the road. Already she was blaming exhaustion, the heat, and frustration. She'd seen something, that was the truth, but Bigfoot? Impossible. No, an animal had crossed her path, that was all. Maybe a bear. Or a big dog. The early summer heat combined with stress had her hallucinating.

"My name's Marnie," she said, taking a step and limping, just a little. Her heels were not meant for running, not even the short distance she'd run back toward this terrible place before settling on a fast walk. "Marnie Somerset."

He looked back and smiled at her. Jeez. Did he have to have a great smile in addition to everything else? "I'm Clint. You look like you could use something to eat, too. Join me?"

She doubted the guy behind the bar would even know what a salad was, much less have one in the kitchen. And if he did, would she want to eat it? Probably not. "Thanks, but I'm not hungry." To immediately prove her a liar, her stomach growled.

Again, that smile. "The usual for me, Harry, and a half club and fries for the lady."

"Coming up." Harry, the rude one, disappeared into a kitchen where he called out the order to… someone.

Marnie gave up, in more ways than one. She limped a few steps and slid onto the bench seat of a booth not far from the bar where the two middle-aged unbearably rude men sat chatting in lowered voices. About her? Probably. She didn't care.

Clint slid in across from her. "What brings you out this way?" he asked. "Lost?"

He had asked that right away, and she'd never answered. Marnie shook her head. "I'm not lost at all, I'm the new Mystic Springs librarian. I'm supposed to start work tomorrow."

Was it her imagination that he drew back from her? No smile, no "welcome to town" no… well, no nothing, other than a suspicious narrowing of his eyes. Blue eyes, she noted. Not that she should note anything.

Harry appeared with two tall glasses of ice water and a scowl. When he was gone, Clint continued, "We're not easy to find. How did you end up here?"

Marnie shrugged, then took a long swig of the water. The ice Harry had neglected to add to her water the first time around made all the difference. She hadn't realized how thirsty she was! When she'd drained half the glass, she set it down, sighed in delight, and answered. "The library in Birmingham where I've been for the past two years had a massive layoff, and I was one of the casualties. I was checking out the want ads and found a listing for the job in Mystic Springs. Since it comes with a place to live, it seemed perfect." She was beginning to think maybe it was not quite so perfect, after all.

She squared her shoulders. There was nothing that said she had to *stay* in Mystic Springs. She'd show up, she'd do her job, she'd give it her best the same way she gave everything her best. If the library was no better than this place, and if the patrons were no friendlier than Harry and his customers, she'd start looking for a new position ASAP.

As an older and attractive — and unlike her boss, *smiling* — woman who'd been hiding in the kitchen all this time delivered their plates, Marnie realized how hungry she really was. The half club and fries were perfect, even though she didn't normally eat bread or fries. Carbs and short women never got along well.

Clint's plate of food was impressive. Not one, but two thick burgers. Fries *and* onion rings. A big bowl of coleslaw. And the waitress, cook, whatever she was said, as she walked away, "I'll get y'all some more water, and I'll have your pie out in a jiffy."

Pie? On top of all that? Now she admired his metabolism as well as his eyes and, well, everything else.

Marnie relaxed a little. Attractive as Clint was, as ripped and chiseled and manly, he was no Mr. Darcy. Before too many years passed, he was going to have a pot belly. He'd probably be bald, too, she threw in for good measure as she whipped a fry through a pile of ketchup on her plate.

God, she had forgotten how good fries were.

For a few moments they both just ate. No talking was necessary as they got down to business. The sandwich was surprisingly good, and Clint seemed to enjoy his burgers well enough.

Hunger somewhat abated, Marnie took a long drink of water and tried to start up a conversation.

"Are you from Mystic Springs?" she asked.

Clint nodded once. Naturally he was the strong and silent type.

"I had never even heard of Mystic Springs, before I saw the job advertised," she said. "Though there are a lot of small towns I've never heard of, I imagine."

This time he shrugged.

She did not, would not, give up. "What can you tell me about the town?" Ha. Let him come up with one word or a gesture to answer *that* question.

He looked directly at her, those blue eyes almost electric, his jaw set. And then he said, in a lowered voice,

"You won't like it."

CHAPTER 2

CLINT TOOK his time changing Marnie Somerset's tire, by the light of a battery-operated lantern he kept in his truck, which was currently parked on the side of the road behind hers. She'd seemed grateful when he'd offered her a ride to her car. As if he would've made her walk. He could've had the job done in ten minutes flat, but he kept stopping to look at her. He stalled, because... hell, he didn't know why.

Squatting down to tighten the lug nuts, he glanced to the side. Her fine legs were right there, so close he could reach out and touch them, though of course he did not. What the hell was a pretty girl like this one doing here? She was a far cry from the previous librarian, in more ways than one.

"I'm afraid you won't find Mystic Springs very exciting," he said as he finished up and stood.

She shrugged. "I'm not necessarily looking for exciting."

He leaned casually against the side of her car. "What are you looking for?"

Her chin lifted, she looked him in the eye. "When I figure that out, I'll let you know."

"Don't expect much in the way of entertainment. Mystic

Springs is a quiet place. We have lots of senior citizens in town," he added. "The town isn't what it once was, but they hang on. Remembering better days, I guess. Most of the younger folks have left town." She wouldn't fit in at all. Let her chew on that a while.

"You're not a senior citizen," she said with a smile.

"No, but I have been known to hang on longer than I should."

The smile turned into a pleasant laugh. He felt that laugh up the length of his spine.

Why was he trying to convince her to leave town before she'd even made it all the way in? She was pretty, she was interesting.

She was bound to be trouble. Strangers always were.

Marnie stopped laughing; her smile faded. She bit her lip for a second or two and turned her head to look into the dark woods. "Have you ever..." Again, she bit her lip.

"Have I ever what?" he prompted.

"Nothing. Never mind. The stress of having a flat tire and the heat have just made me a little crazy. That's all."

He started to tell her she wasn't crazy at all, but thought better of it. It would be best if she started her short time as Mystic Springs librarian thinking she was delusional. It might help later on.

She looked down the dark road. "So, straight ahead until I hit..."

"Main Street," he said when she faltered. "Take a right. The library is four blocks down on your left."

She nodded. "Thanks."

"Good luck with your new job," he said, opening her car door for her, watching as she started the car, rolled down her window and poked her head out to thank him again, and drove away.

Clint climbed into his pickup and followed her for a short distance. Not too closely, but close enough. He turned onto a side road before Marnie reached town, even though he was tempted to make sure she got where she was going without further delay.

He had learned not to give into temptation. It never worked out well. After he made the turn he took a familiar route, past houses dark and well-lit then onto a narrow dirt road just wide enough for this vehicle, to the gravel driveway of his cabin home.

He didn't go inside the cabin after parking the truck. Instead he lifted his head, took a long draw of sweet summer air, and stripped off his clothes.

And then he ran.

Would it be rude to start sending out resumes before she'd even started her new job? She had a few hours…

Marnie gripped the steering wheel tighter than was necessary and leaned slightly forward. She couldn't see much of Mystic Springs downtown as she drove slowly along the narrow main street toward her destination. By the time Clint had changed her tire — he hadn't even worked up a sweat — and given her directions to the library, it had been well past dark. The councilwoman who had hired her had given her simple directions by email, but Marnie was grateful to have those instructions verified. It wasn't long at all before she found herself on Main Street.

Clint's truck had been behind her for a while, as she made her way to town, but at some point he'd turned off. Either that or he drove much more slowly than she did and had fallen way behind, which was unlikely.

Very few lights shone along the way, though she could see evidence of life down side streets to the west, on and around the quaint homes which all seemed to be on that side of downtown proper. Streetlights and front porch lights offered her a dimly lit view of moderate sized homes. Many of them looked older — fifty years or more, she would guess — but were well maintained from all she could tell. Houses yellow and white, pale blue and red brick. She caught sight of a few very large flowering bushes.

Some of the downtown spaces were completely dark, but there were a few lights there as well. Police. Ice cream. A small grocery store. If she'd turned left instead of right she would've run into a small gas station. She saw it in her rearview mirror. All was dark there, too. While there were some lights here and there, there was no discernible activity. She was surprised. It wasn't *that* late.

Clint had warned her that there was a large senior citizen population. Maybe everyone ate at four and went to bed at seven.

To the east things were mostly dark, though she did pass a few short side streets that seemed dimmer than those to the west. The river was on that side of town, on the other side of thick woods. Those woods were completely dark at this time of night. What might be hiding there? Sasquatch? Bears?

The library, which was naturally on the dark side of town, was lit with nothing more than a single bulb near the front door, but at least it was a bright bulb. The front door was glass; the building itself was two stories and constructed of red brick.

There was no other traffic on the street, so Marnie slowly hit the brakes, put her car in park, and opened her purse to draw out the directions to her house.

Naturally, it called for a turn to the left. East. She'd remembered that, but after the stress of the day she wanted to be sure. And yes, she'd recalled the directions correctly, which meant that her house was on the dark side of town. Great.

She drove much more slowly than was necessary. One block past the library, left, then half a block down there it was. Her new home. Well, home for now.

Thank goodness, lights were burning. A bright porch light, as well as at least one inside. Marnie parked in the short driveway, grabbed her overnight bag and laptop case from the back seat, and headed for the front door.

The house was white, the front door dark green. Well-tended flowers bracketed the steps, which squealed a bit as she walked up them. Three steps. The porch squealed, too, but it was an oddly comforting, homey squeal. Home. Yes, this cottage — dark side of town or not — could definitely be home, at least for a while.

As Susan Tisdale had promised, the key to the door was under the mat. *So much for security.*

Marnie unlocked and opened the front door, and for a moment forgot the adventures she'd had making her way here. The interior of her new home was as charming as the exterior. More so, if that was possible. She kicked off her shoes and dropped her bag, and was unexpectedly washed in a feeling of coming home.

It was a small house with a living room — a parlor, she imagined it had always been called — just inside the front door. Her own furnishings had been placed there, along with a few other things. Her couch and matching chair; an ornate coffee table; her knick-knacks on a gleaming walnut bookcase, where some of her books had been mixed with others that had perhaps been left by the previous owner. A padded chair to one side was not hers, but it matched her furniture and suited the room. Fresh flowers, pink and lavender and pale yellow, had been placed in a vase on the coffee table, along with what appeared to be homemade chocolate chip cookies.

She could get used to this.

One cookie in hand, it only took a moment to explore the house. The kitchen was in the very back, and beyond that was a screened-in back porch. She'd have to wait until tomorrow to see what the back yard looked like. It was dark, and she had no desire for another minute of adventure, not even exploring her own back yard. Not tonight. She did wonder if there was, perhaps, a flower garden there. It would definitely be proper for a place like this one. Not that she was much of a gardener. Already she had a plan, of sorts. She could learn to change tires and plant flowers.

Not that watching Clint change her tire for her had been a chore. That man had muscles. And a nice butt. Oh, those arms...

Because she needed to get distracted by a good-looking guy on her first day in town. She did her best to put him out of her mind. There. Done. He was out. Well, kinda.

The kitchen was nicely equipped and well-stocked. There was milk, butter, sliced ham, and eggs in the fridge, oatmeal and raisins and sugar in the pantry. Her own small collection of pots and pans had been stored, her dishes were in the cupboard. In another cupboard there were canned soups, bread, crackers, everything she might need for at least a couple of days.

Sitting next to the coffee maker was a welcoming note from the woman who had hired her, along with a key to the library. Susan Tisdale must be the one responsible for putting the house in order before Marnie arrived. She'd done a fantastic job. The note even included the Wi-Fi password. Ms. Tisdale had forgotten nothing.

The house had two bedrooms and one very nice bath, both on the right side of the house. Her bed had been set up in the back bedroom, which was the largest of the two, and a handful of unpacked boxes were stored in the second bedroom, which faced the street. Not only had her bed been set up, it was made. Her own towels hung on a rack in the bathroom.

All she had to do was shower, put on her pajamas, and crawl into bed. Tomorrow morning, bright and early, she'd check out the library.

First impressions of Mystic Springs aside, if it was even half as charming as this house, she might never leave.

It didn't take long for the light in the back bedroom window to come on. Why in hell had Susan put Marnie in this house? Was she asking for trouble? Looking for it? That wasn't like Susan.

She was a peacemaker, had always been the voice of reason in unreasonable times.

Clint had followed Marnie's scent here, latching onto it and seeking her out, unable to take the chance that he might not see her at least one more time. When strangers came to town they had a tendency not to stay long.

When he'd realized which house she was in, well, he'd been surprised. Maybe there was a reasonable explanation, but he couldn't bring one to mind.

He asked himself, not for the first time tonight, what the hell Susan had been thinking when she'd gone outside the community for a librarian. True, there were a few Non-Springers in town. It was impossible to keep them out. In most cases they didn't stay long, spooked by things they could not explain, feeling like outsiders — which they were — moving on after a short while to places populated with normal people like themselves. A handful had stayed on, either oblivious or accepting, though there were hardcore Springers who would love to send them all packing.

The most militant of the Springers — those who had the blood of the ancestors who'd originally populated Mystic Springs — had gone so far as to scare nosy Non-Springers out of town, on occasion. A couple of them had been difficult to scare, and had discovered the town's secret.

The activities director at The Mystic Springs Retirement Village for the Exceptionally Gifted was a Non-Springer, and so was Mike Benedict's wife. They both knew the truth about this place — how could they not after seeing as much as they had? — and they kept the secret as well as any Springer. They were accepted by most, and would never betray the secrets that abounded here.

But they would always and forever be Non-Springers.

There were a handful of others who'd wandered in and stayed. They either didn't notice the oddities or else didn't care. A new hairdresser. An employee at the grocery store. A couple of retirees who'd been looking to spend their later years in a small, quiet town and had stumbled across the place and a real deal on a nice little house not far from the river. They saw only what they wanted to see, as so many people tended to do.

Mystic Springs was definitely small. It was not so quiet, though.

Someone always kept an eye on these Non-Springers, waiting for the day when they began to notice the magic all around them.

Tempting as she was, Marnie Somerset couldn't stay. They couldn't take the chance that she'd discover the truth. She was too curious, too bright. She wasn't the kind of woman who'd be content to live amidst things she could not explain away. Someone would have to scare her out of town, soon.

Him?

The light in the back window stayed on for a while. He imagined her there, kicking off those ridiculous shoes, unpacking a few things, maybe unwinding a bit before going to bed. The place would be well-stocked for her; she'd have all she needed in the way of food and toiletries to get her through a few days, at least. Susan would have seen to that.

He shouldn't worry about Marnie Somerset. He barely knew her. But after what had happened to the last librarian…

Eventually she turned off the light. Clint waited a few seconds and then he gave a loud whoop.

The light came back on, a curtain fluttered as the new librarian tried to look into the darkness for whatever had made that sound. Clint slipped into the woods, heading for home.

CHAPTER 3

MARNIE WALKED to the library well ahead of the scheduled time to open. Her house was so close, and it was a pleasant morning, so why not? She'd slept well, and had eaten a bowl of oatmeal and drunk a cup of coffee on the screened back porch which, no surprise, looked out over a small but bright flower garden. She noticed a few weeds here and there, but until recently the garden had been well-tended.

There was no sign that a large dog had been in her back yard last night, but beyond a white fence the woods were deep and thick. Her house was — naturally — at the far south edge of town. Anything might be living there. Bears. Wolves. Dogs. *Whatever.*

They had better stay out of her yard.

There were only six houses on her street, three on each side. Her house was sandwiched between two similar cottages. The gray house to the east, nearest to the dead end and the woods beyond, was in desperate need of a coat of paint and a lawn mower. The blue one to the west had been properly maintained, but appeared to be vacant. Both were one-story, with decent sized porches just right for potted plants and rocking chairs, iced tea and neighborly visitors.

The three houses on the north side of the street looked slightly more modern than hers. Two of them — one a boring tan, the other a too-bright blue — had FOR SALE signs planted on recently-mowed lawns. The one that looked lived in was in between those two. It had been painted an inviting pale yellow, and was literally surrounded by flowering bushes.

She'd noticed on the drive in that many of the roads off Main Street had been named for people. Franklin. Smith. Milhouse. Others had flower names, including her own Magnolia Road.

Main Street itself was charming, in a small-town downtown way. There was no rhyme or reason to the style of the individual businesses. It looked as if each had been built independently of the others, then stuck together. The storefronts were white, brick, and all kinds of colors. The styles ranged from modern to quaintly antique. Some looked neglected, while others were well maintained. There were windows small and large, painted and unvarnished. Awnings on some buildings, but not all. One business down the street had a large clay planter by the door, with a beautiful green plant draping onto the sidewalk.

Oddly enough, Main Street ended abruptly a block past Marnie's street. There was a dead end much like the one on her short street, as if the builders had gotten so far and then decided that was far enough.

No one else was out and about at this hour. The businesses along the street were not yet opened, so that was no surprise.

Marnie unlocked the library door, opened it, and stepped inside. She reached to the right and immediately found the light switch there. She flipped it, and overhead lights throughout the library came to life.

She instantly fell in love.

Any doubts she might have had as she'd driven into town last night melted away in a heartbeat. Now, *this* was a library. For a long moment she stood by the door, entranced. Floor to ceiling bookshelves were crammed with books as far as the eye could see. There were no hastily assembled metal shelves here. These bookcases, as well as the front desk, were made of a rich, dark wood that gleamed with polish. The sliding ladder just a few feet away was made of that same wood.

This library was well-loved. It was a dream, a perfect library here in this charming place she hadn't heard of until two weeks ago.

A vase of brightly colored wildflowers had been left on the desk, yet another welcome for her, she supposed. They were similar to the arrangement she'd found waiting in her parlor last night.

She loved the way that sounded. *Her parlor.*

It wasn't yet time to open, so Marnie locked the door behind her and walked to the desk to see if there was a note along with the flowers. There was not. She moved farther into the library, taking slow, deliberate steps. She walked to the nearest section of books and studied the spines. She'd never seen so many fine, well-tended books in one place. And leather! So much leather. She allowed her fingertips to brush the spines of a few books. They were very old, had to be, but many of them looked practically new.

Beyond the front section all the books were neatly arranged, as was proper, but near the desk there was a shelf labeled "popular fiction." The books there included romance, some mystery bestsellers and, of all things, Jane Austen.

"I have found my people," Marnie whispered to an empty room.

Just beyond the shelf of the library's most popular selections there was another, smaller collection of books, a mix of hardbacks and paperbacks. Local Author. Really? *Here?* She glanced at the spine of the closest hardback and tilted her head to read the title and author name. *Bloodlust. JC Maxwell.* She slipped that book from the shelf and recoiled at the image of blood and claw marks on the cover. Ewww. Horror.

Bestselling horror, she noted as she opened the book. There were some impressive quotes on the front page.

She'd never had a stomach for horror novels. Or scary movies or Halloween haunted houses or campfire tales about things that went bump in the night. She closed the book and turned it over to glance at the back cover blurb. Not that she had any intention of reading *Bloodlust*, but if the author was local she might meet him or her.

Him, she noted. Definitely him. The author photo was of a large man in a brown leather jacket. He was impressive. He was handsome. The photographer had coaxed a charming smile out of him. He was apparently not a lumberjack.

JC Maxwell was the man who had changed her tire. Clint.

Seeing his picture brought back the very real horror of her trip into town. Well, maybe horror was a strong word for what she'd been through. By the light of day, and after a surprisingly good night's sleep — her dream about bears and big dogs had been scary but brief, and quickly dismissed after a cup of strong coffee — everything looked different. So she'd had a bit of bad luck on her way to Mystic Springs. It could've happened to anyone. Her cell didn't get a signal on that stretch of road, but she had a full five bars here in town.

The sound she'd heard from those woods last night? A dog, she imagined. A strange, large, perfectly harmless dog who'd probably been more scared than her.

It had definitely not been the creature she'd hallucinated yesterday on her way into town. Nope. No way.

Dog. Maybe some kind of deep-throated bird.

The library opened at nine, six days a week, and closed at five on four of those days. Including Tuesday. She was allowed to close for lunch for up to an hour, though if she preferred she could eat in and remain open during that time. It was an easy enough schedule for one person, and Susan Tisdale had assured her that it was not a demanding job, though the town was proud of its library. With good reason.

Marnie had arrived at the library well before eight, and spent an hour or so familiarizing herself with the system — easy work — and exploring every inch of the impressive facility. There were three computers on an L-shaped desk in the back corner, discretely tucked away public restrooms that appeared to be recently remodeled, and a lovely children's section that not only had many books but also blocks, trains, puzzles, colorful pictures, and small, brightly colored chairs arranged in a semi-circle.

She hadn't had the best luck with children in the past. They were too often noisy and destructive. Her two nephews, ages five and eight, were little terrors who never met a book they didn't think needed to be colored in or torn apart. She would never say so aloud, but they were little shits, like their father. Not that she didn't love her big brother, but as a child he'd broken everything. His kids were just like him. Fortunately she only saw her nephews once or twice a year, and never for very long.

Of course there were the rare children who loved books and enjoyed going to the library, but far too many preferred their electronic devices over the written word on paper, or even on an e-reader. Much as she had tried, she could not compete with video games and texting. Texting! Six-year-olds shouldn't even have cell phones. At least her brother agreed with her on that detail. His kids were, so far, phone-less. The eight year old was addicted to his tablet, which he used exclusively for games and cartoons, *not* for reading e-books. Cretin.

If she ever had children, they would not have cell phones or iPads or any other distracting device which hadn't been invented yet, until they were at least thirteen years old.

Because every kid enjoyed being the only one who didn't have whatever was popular at the time. Which was, she admitted, a worry for another time. Maybe.

Marnie unlocked the front door precisely at nine a.m. She flipped the open/closed sign so that it would show a welcoming OPEN to the street and sidewalk, and waited for the hordes to descend. After all, the library had been closed for several weeks, after the long-time librarian had passed away. She imagined there were books to be returned, and these magnificent shelves were overflowing with stories just waiting to be told. Surely the residents of Mystic Springs were eager to peruse them once again.

This being such a small town, she suspected the residents would be curious about her. She was prepared for scrutiny.

She waited. She'd chosen her outfit specifically for her first day. Skirt flirty, but not too short; heels high, but not her highest by any means; blouse bordering on demure. Her hair waved gently, framing her face.

Marnie stood by the front desk and listened to the clock on the far wall tick, tick, tick as the seconds went past. There were no books to be re-shelved, and the place was so clean she couldn't even busy herself dusting. She had no idea what kind of budget she'd have, so it would be a waste of time to work up a list of books she'd like to buy for these fine shelves.

Maybe sign or no sign, they didn't realize she was here.

At ten on the nose the front door swung open. The bell above the door sounded, a pleasant chime, as an attractive middle-aged woman wearing jeans, a plain blue t-shirt, white tennis shoes, and a wide smile came in. Her brown hair was pulled into a ponytail, and the style accentuated the thinness of her face and the fact that her nose was just slightly crooked. It appeared that she wore not a speck of makeup.

The woman's attention was entirely on Marnie. "There you are! I meant to come by at nine, but it just didn't happen. Busy morning. Welcome to Mystic Springs. I'm Susan Tisdale. We spoke on the phone."

The woman who had hired her, who had left the key under

the mat and had made her house so warm and welcoming, had an infectious smile and intelligent eyes. If it was possible to like a person on sight...

"It's very nice to meet you." Marnie greeted the woman with an outstretched hand. She had so many questions! About the town, about the library, about unusual wild creatures that might live in the area. "Your library is impressive."

Susan smiled. "It's your library, now."

A chill ran up Marnie's spine. *Hers. All hers...* "And the house, the house is just lovely."

"I hope you didn't have any trouble finding your way in. People tend to get lost on the way to our little town."

"I didn't get lost," Marnie said, deciding not to share the tale of her flat tire and her heat-induced hallucination, the unfriendly locals, and the massive man who had come to her rescue. It would sound too much like whining.

"Wonderful!" There was a touch of surprise in her smile.

"Your directions were perfect." Marnie glanced around the room, still awed by the fine collection of books. Why spoil her first impression with complaints? "I didn't expect all this."

"Mystic Springs harbors more than one secret, as all small towns do." Was that a wink? Maybe. "We'll have a welcome reception for you this weekend," Susan said, suddenly all business. "Let's say Friday night, if that suits you, half an hour after closing time." She didn't wait for a response. "I want you to meet the rest of the town council and a few of the library patrons. Oh, and our local author." She smiled.

"I saw the JC Maxwell display when I arrived this morning," Marnie said. "I'm afraid I haven't read any of his work."

"Do read something of his before Friday," Susan instructed. "It will give you nightmares, but since he's local and you'll be meeting him, you really should be familiar with his books."

"Of course." As though she needed help with nightmares. The cover she'd perused, the one with the blood and claw marks, flashed in her memory. A chill much less pleasant than the one she'd experienced when she'd been told that this was *her* library danced down her spine. She was eager to change the subject. "Do the residents of Mystic Springs know I've arrived and the library is open?"

"Oh, yes," Susan said. "They know." She dipped her chin and smiled. "Give them time."

Give them time for what?

Susan conducted a quick and unnecessary tour of the library — Marnie had spent the morning exploring and already knew the place by heart. The tour turned out to be not so unnecessary when Susan opened a door Marnie had assumed was a closet. Okay, so her exploration had been incomplete. Narrow stairs led to what Susan called an office and/or storage closet. There was a table and chair there, a small fridge, a coffee maker — and coffee — and a comfy couch. It was a room meant for napping or eating during lunch break, or perhaps even sleeping in if the weather was bad and she didn't want to walk home in the rain. She was welcome to keep a change of clothes and some toiletries in the closet, in case she decided to spend the night, for weather related reasons or any other.

Any other? Such as...?

After the councilwoman left, Marnie stared at the glass door for several minutes. Fabulous library. Her own house. Flowers and cookies.

It all seemed too good to be true. After the flat tire and her visit to that horrible bar, everything had been perfect. So why did she feel on edge, as if she were waiting for the other shoe to drop?

Relax, Marnie, she told herself. *Relax.*

Clint walked into town, as he often did when the weather was pleasant. It wasn't far, and he enjoyed walking. Anything to get him away from the computer, especially when he was having trouble making a story come together.

He headed to the hardware store, out of curiosity more than anything else. You never knew what Luke might have waiting for you.

The bell over the door sounded as he entered Benedict's Hardware. Luke, situated at the front counter as usual, looked up and smiled. Not that he was surprised to see Clint, or anyone else who shopped here. He was just a friendly guy. A life-long resident of Mystic Springs, Luke Benedict came from a long line of Springers.

Clint didn't understand why Luke didn't have a wife or a girl-friend. He was good-looking enough for a scrawny fella and was always pleasant. He'd dated a cheerleader in high school, but she'd been a Non-Springer who'd left right after graduation. Some in town had been surprised he hadn't followed her.

That had been more than fifteen years ago.

"What have you got for me today?" Clint asked.

Luke reached under the counter and pulled out a small brown bag. "Batteries."

His response was instinctive. "I don't need…"

"Come on, Maxwell, you know the drill. You don't need batteries yet, but you will."

Clint knew better than to argue with Luke. The man knew what he — and everyone else — needed before he did. That was his gift, and a handy one for a man who owned and operated the only hardware store in town. "Put it on my tab."

As Clint reached for the bag, Luke glanced up. "Did you see the new librarian?"

"Yeah. You?"

"Not yet. Think she'll last?"

"As long as no one tries to run her out of town," Clint said under his breath. It happened. Most of the Non-Springers didn't last long. "What have you heard?"

"The usual. A few hardcore Springers want to scare her off and put Lilian Harper in charge of the library."

Clint was mildly horrified. "Can Lilian even read?"

Luke shrugged his shoulders. "I doubt it. But she's one of us, and that's important to some. I don't know why Susan went outside the community with that ad of hers."

Susan had a reason for everything she did. That reason wasn't always clear in the beginning, but in the end...

He should want Marnie gone. He *did* want her gone! She'd seen him. She was curious. Mystic Springs was not a good place to be curious.

There was something interesting about her he couldn't put his finger on. She was pretty, yes, but that wasn't it. There were pretty people everywhere, and Mystic Springs had its share. Marnie Somerset was brave, in a way he'd recognized right away. She'd packed up and come to a new place to... to what? Start over? Find something new? She could definitely find something new here. She might not like it, though.

If she'd found her way to Mystic Springs, she was meant to be here. At least for now.

Clint leaned onto the counter, dipping down so he and Luke were face to face. "No one's to frighten her, no one's to make any attempt to run her off. Spread the word."

Luke didn't look surprised. "Why's that?"

"I have my reasons." He gave a cryptic answer because he couldn't explain his motivations, not even to himself. The librarian deserved a chance. If she decided not to stay it should be her own decision. She shouldn't be forced out.

And if anyone was going to scare her away, when the time came, it would be him.

CHAPTER 4

No one came into the library. No one. Once Marnie had familiarized herself with the layout and the system, there was nothing much to do. She'd spent a couple of hours in the afternoon reading Clint's book, just to kill time. She chose the hardback with the claw marks on the cover, which was one of five titles. Less than a quarter of the way in she slammed the book shut and returned it to the shelf.

Disembowelment and splattered brains did not make for pleasant reading. She *liked* pleasant reading.

At the end of her first day as librarian, Marnie locked the front door as she left, wondering as she did so why she bothered. It wasn't like she expected after-hours visitors. Was it her or was it the place? Did these people hate books or were they wary of the new librarian?

Standing on the sidewalk outside the library, she got a better look at Mystic Springs than she had on her way in that morning. She'd noticed the buildings themselves, but not so much what was in them. She eyed the pair of eateries directly across the street, a bakery and cafe that looked to be designed to complement one another. One brick storefront was accented in teal, the other in purple. The signs in both windows were perfectly lettered. In teal, Eve's Cafe. In lavender, Ivy's Bakery. There were matching awnings.

On either side of Eve's and Ivy's were other red-brick fronted shops. Though not so colorfully embellished as the two businesses directly across from the library, they looked welcoming enough. One was a hardware store. The other seemed to be a boutique. Colorful clothing was displayed in the window. And oh, were those shoes?

Those four businesses formed one side of a charming city block.

There were a few people on that side of the street, coming and going, talking to one another at the end of the day, laughing at jokes she could not hear.

Marnie gathered her courage, such as it was. If they wouldn't come to her, she'd go to them. Maybe if she introduced herself, if she smiled and invited the locals into her library — and yes, it was already hers — they'd make a point of stopping by.

Her stomach growled as she crossed the street. Susan — or someone — had stocked Marnie's house well. Marnie had eaten oatmeal and a banana for breakfast but she'd skipped lunch, sure that if she ran out for a bite someone would stop by. Someone, anyone…

She glanced at one business and then the other. Did she want cake or a salad? Cake, of course, especially after the day she'd had. Maybe a cupcake like the one painted on the window. She headed for the bakery, and had almost reached her destination when the purple neon OPEN sign went dark. A shade came down over the glass-front door, and there was a decidedly loud click as a deadbolt was slammed into place. Marnie pulled her phone from her pocket and checked the time. Five-eleven couldn't be the normal closing time. Had the bakery stayed open late or closed early? There were no hours posted on the front window, so it was impossible to tell.

Marnie turned to the cafe, half expecting the same thing to happen. The light would go dark, the door would be locked...

Hours of operation had been painted on the cafe's glass door: Eleven a.m. to seven p.m. six days a week, closed on Sunday. There were also customers visible through the front window. Marnie opened the door and walked into the cafe, breathing a sigh of relief as the aromas hit her. *Oh My God*, something smelled good.

It was not a salad.

She ignored the fact that the half dozen patrons stared — make that glared — at her as she walked to a booth and sat. Okay, it was a small town and she was a stranger. *Glare all you want, people*, she thought as she plucked a menu from its place between the napkin dispenser and a ketchup bottle. *I'm hungry and will not be denied.*

A redhead came to the edge of the table, order pad in hand. Marnie looked up, half expecting the waitress to be grimacing or scowling. She was relieved to find the attractive woman smiling warmly.

"Hey there, you must be the new librarian."

Sigh. A normal greeting! "I am. Marnie Somerset." She offered her hand. She'd stand, but the waitress was too close to the end of the seat. Knocking her down would not be the best way to start.

"Eve Franklin," the woman said as she took Marnie's hand and shook it briefly. "This is my place." She nodded once. "What can I get you?"

Marnie glanced at the menu. "I should get a salad, I had really planned to get a salad." Her meal of choice, most days. "But what is that that smells so good?"

"My special of the day, Granny's meatball stew."

There would be plenty of salads in days to come. It had been a strange couple of days, and Marnie wanted whatever had created that wonderful aroma. "I'll have that, and a glass of sweet tea."

Eve nodded and was off. Some of the other diners still stared, but a couple of them had returned to their meals and private conversations. They'd get used to her, Marnie decided as she waited for her food. She nodded and smiled to one older woman who continued to study Marnie with narrowed eyes and thinned lips. The woman's head snapped down and she began to eat.

The front door opened, and like everyone else, Marnie looked to see who had arrived.

The woman who walked in gave Marnie a start. She was identical to Eve, who had taken her order and disappeared into the kitchen. Except this woman wore a purple apron with the words Ivy's Bakery printed across the bosom, and her long red hair was pulled up into a messy bun. Ivy looked good in a messy bun. Marnie had tried that style in the past, when her hair had been longer. Somehow she'd always ended up looking homeless.

Instead of offering a friendly smile, this woman glanced Marnie's way with thunder in her eyes and disapproving pursed lips.

She might never get a cupcake…

Eve approached with a tray bearing a huge bowl and two glasses of tea. She placed the stew — which smelled even better up close than it had as she'd entered the place — before Marnie. The tea came next. The second glass of tea was placed on the other side of the table. Eve took a seat and lifted that tea to her lips. After a smile and a sigh, she urged Marnie to eat.

And she did. She was so hungry, the stew seemed to be the best thing she'd ever eaten. What was that flavor? It was… flavor.

After a while it hit her. The stew tasted like a weird combination of Nannie's chicken and dumplings and her Mom's lasagna — a favorite from childhood, when her parents had still been together — and a pot roast her Aunt Sally had made once, for a rare family reunion.

A flood of memories hit her. Memories of long-ago meals shared with family, of laughter around the dining room table. The emotions connected to those memories were strong, and they flooded through her as strongly as the flavors had. The aromas and flavors of Thanksgivings shared with family. Christmas Eve, with her parents and brother, before everything had fallen apart. Not just the tastes of family traditions, but the emotions. The joy. Tears filled her eyes, but she continued to eat.

"The first time it's always like this," Eve said. "Just eat. Next time will be easier."

Marnie looked up. She had almost forgotten Eve was there! "I'm sorry. I don't understand."

Eve waved a dismissive hand, and then spoke to the young waitress who had taken over for her, giving instruction about preparations for closing up in a little more than an hour. The girl nodded, cut a suspicious glance to Marnie, and scurried off.

The woman who had created the masterpiece Marnie was enjoying took a long swig of tea, then said, "I suppose you've noticed that Mystic Springs is a little odd."

Marnie dabbed at her mouth with a napkin before responding. "A little odd? I feel like I've wandered into *The Twilight Zone*."

Eve laughed. It was a good laugh, real and deep. Her eyes almost sparkled. "I imagine it does. This is a very small and tight-knit town, and some of the residents are a bit old fashioned. Stuck in their ways, I suppose, and not fans of any kind of change. It takes the people here a while to warm up to strangers. Give us a chance, and if it's meant to be all will be well."

"And if it's not meant to be?"

Eve's smile faded. "Then all won't be well."

A chill walked down Marnie's spine. Was that a threat? From this seemingly lovely and friendly woman? It sure felt like a threat. Maybe moving in with her dad until she found another job wasn't such a bad idea after all. Claudia, her newest stepmother, would baby her for a while, until she got tired of having her husband's grown daughter underfoot. Her dad would try to get her to go back to school for a degree in something other than library science, which was always annoying, but still...

"A few words of advice," Eve said. The smile was back, and it seemed genuine enough. "You can drive out of town for groceries and such, but people notice these things. You could also order online, but to be honest only about half the packages arrive. The UPS man is always getting lost. Once we found a stack of packages tossed to the side of the road." She shook her head at the memory. "If you want to stay here, if you plan to become a part of the community, you need to shop local. There's a small grocery store two blocks down. They don't have much, but they do have the basics and they can order in anything you want. Same with clothes. There's the boutique next door, and a different kind of shop just down from the grocery store. Between the two, they'll have or can get anything you want."

"That makes sense," Marnie said. Nothing Eve had said could be considered a threat. It had just been a couple of very long days. That was the only explanation for the fleeting feeling that there was any kind of warning in the woman's words. She paused the conversation to take another bite of the weirdly delicious stew.

The woman from the bakery had taken a seat at the counter. It was impossible not to notice how she glared.

Marnie didn't look in that direction as she asked, "The woman from the bakery, is she your sister?" Sister or angry clone? Had to be one or the other.

"Ivy's my twin. She's not much of a fan of outsiders, as you might have noticed. She'll come around. Maybe."

That *maybe* was telling. Yeah, no cupcakes for her, not in the near future, anyway.

"One other thing," Eve began, a new hint of something uncertain in her voice. She paused. She chewed her bottom lip.

"Just say it," Marnie said. "At this point nothing would surprise me."

The slight lift of Eve's eyebrows hinted otherwise. After a short pause she said, "Don't go out after dark."

Marnie walked slowly down the sidewalk, away from the cafe and a woman she might, one day, be able to call a friend. It was too early to be sure.

Walking not toward home but away, she glanced in windows and crossed side streets, taking a moment here and there to look at the houses down those streets. Quite a few appeared to be empty, but in some cases it was hard to tell. She did see an occasional "For Sale" sign here and there. Some of them had been in place so long they were faded. Others leaned ominously to one side, much as the Welcome to Mystic Springs sign had.

Now and then she saw people up ahead, but by the time she reached that point they were gone. Coincidence, or were they actively avoiding her? She crossed Main Street in front of the Mystic Springs Police Station, and walked back the way she'd come, studying the businesses that were on the same side of the street as the library. An ice cream parlor and a beauty salon, side by side. The grocery store, which looked, with a glance through the wide glass windows, to be very well stocked for one so small. An antique store that seemed to be bursting at the seams. The other shop that sold clothing, which was closed at this time of day. That was the store that kept a large plant by the door, one so large Marnie had to adjust her path to skirt around it.

She reached the library and continued on a short distance. At the end of the street, the dead end of Main Street, the trees were thick. It was odd that the main thoroughfare simply ended, without warning, without even a narrow side street in one direction or another.

Marnie didn't like the look of those woods. They were too dense, too dark. It was a relief to make the turn down her own Magnolia Road.

It was almost dark. Not quite, but the skies were gray, and the woods at the far end of the street were getting there. She could see nothing beyond the entrance to the woods. Maybe she'd find a pathway there, if she were to look for one. Surely there was. She should be able to walk down to the river, check out what might lie on the other side of those woods, but that kind of exploring was best done in broad daylight.

Eve's advice about staying in after dark remained with her. That warning had all but frozen Marnie. Why hadn't she asked more questions? She was filled with them. Were there wild dogs? Likely. That's what she'd seen and heard last night. A huge wild dog. That walked on two legs. She'd seen trained dogs do that, but they were usually small. And none of them had *looked* at her…

Marnie grabbed her keys and unlocked her front door with more urgency than was necessary. When she was inside, she locked the door behind her and sighed in relief.

Maybe she'd call her dad tonight, see if he'd mind moving his exercise equipment out of her old bedroom for a while. She couldn't, wouldn't, call her mother. Not only was she too far away, her husband didn't care for kids. Not even fully-grown ones. Marnie hadn't had a close relationship with her mother for so long she barely remembered what it had been like. The occasional phone call or email, birthday and Christmas cards. That was it. There would be no help there.

That odd feeling of being home washed over Marnie. No. She wouldn't call her dad. Not yet. She had one maybe-friend in Eve, and surely there were others who wouldn't entirely reject an outsider.

What was this, a 17th century village where the people were isolated from the outside world? Where strangers were distrusted? Where anyone different was called a witch and burned at the stake and…

Nonsense. After four years in Birmingham, she just wasn't accustomed to small-town life.

In the safety of her home, she relaxed. Then, because she couldn't be sure who had lived here before and who might have a key, she locked the front door and jammed one of the wooden kitchen chairs under the doorknob. Just in case.

She went to the screened-in back porch and looked out over her back yard, admiring her very own beautiful flower garden. Night fell slowly across the well-tended yard, as well as the wooded and over-grown landscape on the other side of the fence. All of it, the tamed and the wild, was beautiful and enchanting. If she was at all artistic, she would be inspired to paint the scene. Maybe she'd take a bunch of pictures with her phone. She wasn't a great photographer, but if she took enough pictures surely some of them would turn out. It would be nice to have something to remember this place by, after she fled like the devil was on her tail. Which she likely would, sooner or later.

Movement in the brush beyond her yard caught her eye. Deer, maybe. Wild dogs. A bear.

It stepped out from behind a tree, tall and hairy, standing on two feet, and looking directly at her. One long and hairy arm lifted slowly, then lowered again, almost as if it was *waving* to her. The thing seemed to shuffle its feet, though it did not move closer, or away. A bushy head cocked to one side as the animal — beast, monster, impossible being — studied her.

Marnie held her breath. This was not possible. That thing couldn't exist. She wanted to reach for her phone and try to take a picture, but night was falling fast and besides, the creature would be gone before she could grab her cell, she knew it.

So she held her breath and stared, afraid even to blink. This time there was no mistake, no hallucination. What she was looking at was real. It was undeniable.

She'd found Bigfoot.

———

There had been a time when Springer meetings had been held in the library. Tonight, they gathered in Susan Tisdale's house, a big, rambling mini-mansion that was likely the oldest building in town. Her parents had lived here, and so had her grandparents and great-grandparents, who had built this house more than a hundred years ago. Susan's front parlor was the largest downstairs room, and that was where the Springers met.

The meeting was already in chaos when Clint walked into the room. That's what he got for being twenty minutes late. Susan was in the middle of it, under attack by a dozen or so — the hardliners — for bringing in an outsider for a job as crucial as running the library. She tried to reason with them, but was having no luck.

A dozen or so stood, while a handful of others had claimed ancient seats around the parlor. Those chairs and sofas were as old as the house.

Clint put two fingers to his lips and let out a whistle that silenced them all, and had a few covering their ears. When he had everyone's attention, he spoke.

"Susan's right. We need new blood. Let's face it, too many of us are related, in some way or another. There aren't enough kids in town to justify keeping the school open, and have you seen how many homes are for sale?" Some who died or moved on left their houses to the city, knowing they'd never sell. "In a few years we'll all be in the old folks' home, and…"

"The Alabama Home for the Exceptionally Gifted not an old folks' home, it's a retirement community!" A resident of said home called out indignantly, from his perch on a pale green fainting couch. The sign in front of the three-story building read Mystic Springs Retirement Village, but no one called it that. The residents called it The Alabama Home for the Exceptionally Gifted. Everyone else called it The Egg.

"We need new blood," Clint said again.

"You planning to eat her?" Donnie Milhouse, the middle of Harry's five boys, called out with a cackle.

Clint just glared. They all knew he was a vegetarian when he shifted.

The youngest of the Milhouse boys, red-headed Weston, chimed in. "I hear she's pretty. Is that why you want her to stay?"

Eve, who'd been standing at the far end of the room observing the commotion instead of participating in it, called out, "I like her."

Her sister said, in a sour voice, "I don't."

"You didn't even talk to her," Eve argued. "I think we should give her a chance. It's not like we don't know how to deal with her if she becomes a problem."

A few hardliners agreed. Most did not.

Yes, they could deal with her, if it became necessary. Amnesia punch and a ride to the edge of town, or a big slice of Frannie's funeral cake?

Luke entered the parlor. He was late, too, but had obviously been listening. "You all know what I do. When you need something, I know it before you do. You come into my store and I have whatever you need waiting for you. Maybe it's a screwdriver, or a replacement battery, or a plunger for a toilet that's going to need one in a day or two. This is different, and I understand there are some of you who won't agree with me, but…"

"But what?" Ivy snapped when he hesitated.

"Mystic Springs needs the librarian."

Clint breathed a sigh of relief. Even the hardliners listened to Luke. If he had them on his side…

Donnie Milhouse spoke up again. "Maybe we do and maybe we don't. Until I know for sure, I'd feel better if someone kept a close eye on her."

Several Springers nodded in agreement. A number of names, hardliners all, were shouted out and shouted down. Most of them would be more of a danger to Marnie than an asset. They'd keep an eye on her until she did something they didn't like, and then all bets would be off.

"Eve and Ivy are right across the street from the library," Clint began, but a gruff voice interrupted.

"I live right next door."

Clint stared at James Garvin, a too-quiet man who was one of the worst of the Springers. For good reason, perhaps. His wife had been dead for close to twenty years. His sons had left town not long after. Neither of them had returned to visit their widowed father, not even for a day. James managed to find a way to blame everyone and everything for his wife's death and his sons' desertion. He blamed everyone but himself.

A long-time resident of The Egg shouted out, "Clint Maxwell, you had dinner with her at Harry's bar, and you fixed her damn tire. You welcomed her to town, when you should have been running her off."

They'd been talking about Marnie long before this meeting had gotten underway. It was difficult to keep secrets here.

"I nominate Maxwell as babysitter for the librarian," the older man continued, raising his bushy eyebrows. And then he smiled. "Until we decide what to do with her."

CHAPTER 5

Marnie had an early breakfast — oatmeal again — and rushed out her front door and down the steps more than an hour before the library was scheduled to open. Not that it was likely to be any busier than it had been yesterday, but she'd been seen around town so maybe a few would drop by. Maybe. She'd be ready for whatever the day might bring.

Last night, after dark — and after double checking that all doors and windows were locked — she'd settled on the sofa in her parlor, opened up her laptop, and started her search. Bigfoot. She found a lot of information, but for the most part the internet was a million miles wide and a quarter of an inch deep. After an hour and a half, she gave up the search. There was too much information, and none of it struck her as being reliable.

Yes, she was looking for reliable information on a mythical creature. A *supposedly* mythical creature she'd seen just beyond her own back yard fence. She needed books. Research books on Bigfoot. Yeti. Sasquatch. Whatever you wanted to call him. Him or it? Again, whatever.

There were a handful of people on the street this morning, a couple of them headed to Ivy's, others down the street near the grocery store. Yesterday the bakery had been dark, but this morning the purple OPEN sign was lit. Marnie waved, not at anyone in particular but in the general direction of Ivy's. No one waved back, though they had to have seen her. She wouldn't allow them to completely ignore her. She waved again, more vigorously this time, and smiled widely. That led to a number of people deciding to stare down at the sidewalk.

At least she knew she'd been seen.

There was someone new on the street; someone Marnie didn't notice until she reached the library door. A little girl, maybe eleven or twelve years old she'd guess, stepped onto the main street from a side road. She skipped, and blonde pigtails danced. The child wore baggy shorts and a pale green t-shirt, as well as white tennis shoes. Dressed for a lazy summer day, the girl smiled as if everything was right with the world. For her, maybe it was.

Marnie paused a minute and watched. There was such joy on the little girl's face.

As if she knew she was being watched, the child looked at Marnie and — hallelujah — she waved before darting past an older couple and slipping into the bakery.

Surely the child got a better reception there than Marnie had.

She was disappointed — but not surprised — to find that the library only had a handful of books on Bigfoot. All but one was at least twenty years old. Of course there weren't a lot of books on the subject. There weren't many on unicorns, either, or mermaids. She decided to start with the oldest book first and move forward, saving the newest book for last. It was less than three years old, and a real find.

Last night she'd been tempted to email a couple of friends in Birmingham and tell them about Bigfoot, but in the end she had not. They'd think she'd lost her mind, that losing her job and the breakup with Jay had combined to unhinge her. Never mind that the split with Jay had been her idea and that she'd found this job right away. No, she needed proof first. A photo, maybe. A hair, so she could check the DNA? Ha, no. She did not intend to get close enough to pluck out a long Bigfoot hair.

There were quite a few photos that had been taken over the years, out of focus, blurry, indistinct photographs. Most had been deemed fake. But were they?

What she'd seen last night had not been fake. She could not blame the sighting on heat exhaustion or stress or the discomfort of a sweaty bra, not this time.

There was little in this world that Marnie liked better than research. She had her books, a notebook with a pretty cover, and three pens, in case one or two dried out as she took notes. She did keep an eye on the time, though. She shouldn't be late unlocking the doors on her second day. At two minutes to nine, she set her research books aside and walked to the door, key in hand. Yesterday she'd waited all day for patrons. Today she kind of hoped no one came in, so she could continue her research uninterrupted.

When she had more details, she'd go back to the internet and restart that search with more information in hand. That would guide her to where she needed to be. Books would set her on the right path. They always did.

At five after nine, well before she could get back into her book, the door opened. She expected it might be Susan again, but when she caught a glimpse of red hair, she was certain it was Eve.

A sour expression and a purple apron — did she ever take it off? — told her it was Ivy. The baker who'd closed up shop on Marnie last night. The pretty woman with the impressive scowl.

Ivy sighed as she approached. It was a long-suffering type of sigh, accompanied by a disapproving frown. "I've been told to give you a chance. Here." She plopped a smallish wicker basket on the counter. The contents were covered with a lavender napkin.

What was in that basket? Cookies or snakes? Maybe a poisonous spider or two. Maybe all three.

Marnie very cautiously lifted one corner of the napkin and peeked inside. Muffins, cinnamon judging by the scent. Cookies. Chocolate chip, her favorite. Some sort of chocolate covered ball. Candy, maybe, or a fancy kind of cookie. It all looked delicious. But were these goodies safe to eat?

As if she'd read her mind, Ivy reached into the basket without looking and grabbed a cookie. She took a big bite, and again she sighed. "I'm a good baker. If I was going to poison you it would not be through one of my own creations. I'd put something in your coffee or slip a nasty drug into a dish my sister served you."

"Great," Marnie mumbled.

"You're safe, for now." Ivy waited, obviously wanting Marnie to eat something from the basket. Since she wasn't really hungry, she went for one of the smallish balls. What the hell? Why not?

She popped the ball into her mouth and bit down.

The sensation was similar to the one she'd experienced last night, as she'd eaten Eve's stew. The burst of flavor was outrageous. Raspberry and dark chocolate, her favorite dessert combination. Mostly the chocolate, but with the raspberry combined… Yum. She reached into the basket for another.

"I am going to gain so much weight with you right across the street," she said as she ate another.

For the first time, at least that she'd seen, Ivy smiled. "No, you won't. My treats come without calories."

Marnie laughed. Maybe Ivy wasn't so bad after all. At least she had a sense of humor. Some people took time to warm up to strangers, to make friends, to smile. Or at least not glare. Was it at all possible that Ivy might one day actually be a friend? It definitely seemed like a long shot.

As casually as she could manage, Marnie said, "I tried to stop by last night, but I missed you. When is your bakery open?"

"When I feel like it."

That was not helpful, not at all. Marnie had a feeling the answer hadn't been meant to be helpful.

Ivy turned on her heel and headed for the exit. Okay, she wasn't as friendly as her sister. She might be a complete psycho. It was too early to tell.

But damn, she could cook.

"Thanks!" Marnie called out. Ivy didn't respond.

When she was alone again Marnie ate another of the treats, a cookie this time, and in the process almost forgot about her research.

Almost.

Clint hadn't had a house phone for years. He'd kept it for a while after his parents had passed, but service had always been unreliable. Any calls that had managed to come through on that number had been telemarketers or out and out scams. If someone in town could come up with a spell to block those calls, they'd make a fortune. Everyone used his cell, and that way he could be reached no matter where he was. He occasionally traveled for research and was sometimes away for days at a time.

When his cell rang, his immediate response was annoyance. The book he was working on was overdue. Not by a lot, but he hated to be late. With this book, he was definitely late.

Ivy's name popped up on the screen, so he answered. She wouldn't stop calling; she hated to be ignored.

"Yup," he said into the phone.

"She's investigating you," Ivy said, her voice cool and clipped.

He didn't have to ask who. "What makes you say that?"

"I was trying to be nice, like everyone said I should. *Give her a chance. She's not so bad. Get to know her.*" Ivy's voice was apparently meant to be a whiny impression of her sister, who in all honesty sounded exactly like her so no change in tone was necessary. "I took her a welcome basket of treats."

"You're not trying to poison her, are you?"

"No. Why does everyone think that? Sheesh. Poison one person, and from that day forward everyone assumes…" She sighed. "I really am trying, I swear. For now. Look, the cutesy librarian was sitting at the front desk with a stack of books. I couldn't see the titles of all, but at least two were about you."

Not JC Maxwell, author, he knew. That sort of research wouldn't be cause for alarm. "She saw me," he confessed. *Twice.* "She'll poke around and find nothing, and then she'll move on. Sooner or later something else will grab her attention."

"Or else she'll leave, which would be even better. I don't care what Luke says, we don't need her. We don't need any outsiders."

He didn't try to argue with her. It would be a waste of breath. Ivy had had a bad experience with a Non-Springer. Four years had passed, but she didn't seem to be anywhere near letting it go. "What do you want me to do?"

"I want you to scare her out of town, but judging by the way you defended her last night, that's not going to happen. If she was twenty years older and not so pretty, I bet you'd be glad to scare her off. The least you can do is keep an eye on her, as you've been instructed to do."

"She can research all she wants, she won't find anything."

Ivy gave into one of her long-suffering sighs, which was plenty loud enough for Clint to hear. As she'd certainly intended. "It would be best if her attentions were elsewhere. I have to go. My cookies are going to burn. Dammit!"

With that Ivy ended the call. Clint cursed as he set his phone aside. Mystic Springs' baker never burned anything.

The call had completely pulled him out of the chapter he'd been working on. The idea for the scene had vanished, which meant it had probably been crap to begin with. What the hell? He could use a little distraction, and the new librarian would definitely make a pleasant diversion. He grabbed a book and headed for the front door.

The walk from his house — an eighteen hundred square foot

upscale cabin in the woods just south of Mystic Springs proper — to town was just under two miles, and was a nice enough walk most of the year. In the worst heat of summer, which had not yet arrived, those two miles could be miserable, even for him. During those hellish days of summer he drove, taking the dirt road from the back of his cabin to the edge of town, down a side road to Main Street. Today the air was warm, but nowhere near miserable. The thick trees that lined the path kept the temps cool enough. He was tempted to strip down here and now and go for a run. A wild and free run in his natural state. But he didn't.

It had taken a long while — years — but unlike his father, Clint had complete control of his abilities. He could feel the shift coming on; he could experience that tickle down his spine, acknowledge it, and then push the urge back. He was in control; there was power in taking command of such a powerful gift.

When he was away from Mystic Springs that command faded, over a period of a few days or even a couple of weeks. The drive to embrace the beast became stronger, which necessitated that he plan his public appearances carefully. He had to be able to get away at a moment's notice.

If he stayed away long enough, his ability to shift would disappear entirely. He was never away from home any longer than he had to be.

Bigfoot. Yeti. Sasquatch. He and his kind had been called a lot of names over the years. So far no one outside a small circle realized that like a werewolf, or any were animal, Bigfoot was a shifter. Some of them, at least.

His control had improved significantly since high school, when the change had come more frequently, quicker, and often without warning. The nicknames the other kids had stuck him with in those years… the way the girls had laughed… those were not pleasant memories.

It wasn't like he was the only shifter in Mystic Springs. The Milhouses were werewolves, but for some reason that was seen as being cooler than Clint's own gift. Their shift was tied to the moon, they changed on a damn schedule, so they'd never embarrassed themselves in high school. They hadn't been laughed at.

He'd had little control, those first couple of years, which had led to a handful of embarrassing high school moments. Sprouting hair during a stressful test, or growling in answer to a teacher's question had not gone over well. By the time he was a senior things had been better, but it wasn't as if the others didn't remember, as if they didn't know what he was.

He'd thought his high school girlfriend — and eventually wife — Jenna was different, but discovering that she'd made it her life's purpose to change him had rocked his world, for a while. He could thank her for that, in a twisted way. Until he'd found out Jenna wanted to take away that part of him, he hadn't realized how important it was.

It was true. His ex-wife was a real witch.

There were many names for what he — and his father and grandfather and great-grandfather — was. Every culture had a Bigfoot legend, which made him wonder how many like him there were in the world. Were they truly like him, or were they always in their animal form? He had no way of knowing.

His father had preferred to call himself and his son Dyn Gwallt, rather than Bigfoot. Clint had always thought that sounded much more exotic than any of the other names he'd heard, until he'd found out Dyn Gwallt was simply Welsh for Hairy Man. Given that it was Welsh, his father — and he — had probably been mispronouncing the words, but Clint had no desire to amend that. Butchered as it was, Dyn Gwallt was his father's word, and now was his. What difference did it make if it was mis-pronounced? He was likely the last of his kind, at least in this line of Maxwells. He didn't see children in his future, especially not with the health of Mystic Springs itself in danger.

Those shifters who'd left Mystic Springs would've eventually lost their abilities. He imagined raising a seemingly normal child in a normal world would be easier than the isolation being a Springer required. Maybe subsequent generations didn't even know what they were, or rather what they would be if they were here. If they were home.

He considered himself lucky. His father had never found any control. Had never particularly wanted control. With him the shift had always come without warning. They could be eating dinner, and his dad would begin to sprout long hairs on his face. A grunt and a curse word later, Terrence Maxwell was out the door, stripping off his clothes as he went.

Clint's mother, a Springer herself and a cousin to Eve and Ivy's mother, had been blessed with the patience of a saint.

His parents had been gone just over four years. A car wreck had killed them both. They never should've left Mystic Springs, not even for a day.

There had been several other shifters in town over the years, but as far as he knew all but the Milhouses had moved on. The others had deserted Mystic Springs, as so many had.

Clint walked past a row of small houses at the edge of town, through an overgrown garden, past a couple of vacant houses and onto the end of the downtown street. Everything he needed was here. There was no reason to ever leave Mystic Springs again. But he would, when he got antsy, when the place began to wear on him, when he craved a break from his reality. When he felt the need to do some in-person research. After a short while away he would return. He always did.

At thirty-four years old, he was a successful author. He had friends; some here in the town where he'd been born and others — authors, editors, an agent — far away. Most of the long-distance friends he'd never met face to face. They communicated through email/cell phone/social media. They were a part of another life, a life he could never fully embrace. Clint was often invited to visit New York, or to stay at a writer friend's house, or to speak at a conference. He rarely accepted those invitations.

His outsider friends all thought he was terribly introverted. One had accused him, laughingly, of being paranoid. None of them suspected the truth, and they never would.

Eyes on the library, Clint crossed the street. The lack of people out and about was evidence that Mystic Springs was dying. Slowly, one death or departure at a time. When he'd been a boy, the downtown street had been busy all day. People shopped and ate and laughed. They visited and spent money and hung out at the library. He couldn't count the hours he'd spent in that library; as a child, as a young man, as an adult. It had always been a place of peace, of refuge.

At the moment there were four people on the street. Four. In an hour or so there would be more, as residents went to Eve's to eat, but still it would be nothing like it had once been.

Luke said the town needed Marnie Somerset. Clint wasn't sure about that — people weren't Luke's specialty, after all — but he had to give her a chance.

She had to give Mystic Springs a chance.

Marnie jumped when the bell over the entrance pinged. Finally! Someone who wanted a book! Her joy faded a moment later, as Clint approached the desk with an obviously forced smile on his face.

"How's it going?" he asked.

She gathered her stack of books and placed them on a lower shelf, out of sight. The notebook joined them. She didn't want the local author to think she was a nut job. "Fine!" she said too brightly, and then she sighed. "And I admit, much too slow. This is such a great library. Why don't more people use it?" She stood and glanced around. "If I'd lived near a library like this one when I was growing up, I never would've left it."

She noticed that he had a hardback book in his hand. As she

glanced at it, he lifted the book and handed it to her. "My newest release. I always donate a copy to the library."

Marnie smiled and took the book from his hands, glancing down at the cover. *Wolf's Curse*. A silhouette. A blood moon. Glowing eyes in the darkness, and yes, those were claws. Great.

He read the expression on her face too well. Clint — JC Maxwell — grinned and said, "You don't have to read it. Horror isn't for everyone."

She clasped the book to her chest. "I'm so sorry. I tried to read one of your books yesterday, and not even fifty pages in it scared the bejesus out of me. It gave me nightmares!"

His grin — it was a very nice grin, she conceded — widened. "Good. I did my job."

"It's your job to scare people into insomnia and night terrors."

"Yep."

She chewed on her lower lip for a moment, then bravely asked, "Why not mysteries, or political thrillers, or romance?"

"Romance?"

"Why not?"

His eyes narrowed, a little. "Why aren't you an accountant? Or a doctor? Or a professional wrestler?"

"I never wanted anything but…" She smiled, too. "Okay, sorry I asked. We are what we are, I suppose."

His smile faded, but just a little. "There's truth in that. Can I buy you lunch?"

Well, that invitation came out of nowhere. She tried not to stammer and failed.

"I'm not asking you on a date," he clarified. "I'm hungry. You're here. It's lunchtime. Let me welcome you to town with a meal."

"You've already fed me once *and* changed my tire. That's welcome enough."

"Let me buy you a pleasant meal, on a better day."

She shouldn't be hungry, but she had managed to lay off Ivy's goodies for the past couple of hours. And it would do her good to get to know more of the locals. And dammit, Clint was all man and looking at her like she was all woman, even though she knew she should lose fifteen pounds and she had her father's nose and…

"Just lunch, Marnie," he said in a calming voice that managed to cut right through her. "Just lunch."

It wasn't like anyone else would arrive any time soon needing an emergency library book, and Susan had told her she could close for lunch.

Two minutes later she replaced the OPEN sign on the door with one that read BACK IN THIRTY MINUTES. She'd always hated those particular signs. They were imprecise. If you didn't know what time a place had closed, how could you possibly know when half an hour had passed?

She was worrying too much. Just lunch, he said. What did she have to lose?

CHAPTER 6

EVE'S WASN'T ENTIRELY empty, but damn, it wasn't packed, either. Marnie glanced around, hoping to spot a friendly face or two. Nada. Susan Tisdale was the only friendly face she'd seen since coming to Mystic Springs. Eve seemed friendly, but she was a business owner wooing a customer. Did that count?

She had a reason for hoping Eve's business was good at the present time. It would be easier to chitchat in a crowd, carrying on one conversation among many in a busy cafe. But no. There was a single old man at the counter, and two women at a table in the corner. That was it.

The customers, all three of them, stared. She had to admit, Clint was definitely stare-worthy. Then again, she was still a stranger in town. Maybe they were staring at her, as others had last night. The old man was definitely looking at her; he gave her the willies, with his narrowed eyes and scowl. The ladies, who both appeared to be in their forties, were probably staring at the man who had invited Marnie to lunch. And why not? He was yummy, and as she had already noted, definitely worthy of an admiring once-over, or two.

Marnie had met plenty of authors in the past. Local

romance authors, historians, a couple of YA authors. They'd come into the Birmingham library for talks, readings, and book-signings. She'd liked almost all of them — there had been one exception, and that poor woman might've simply been having a bad day — but then it was easy to like another book lover. In all that time, she'd never met an author whose mind was so twisted. Would a normal man be driven to write about the kind of violence that was in Clint's books? Seriously, what was *wrong* with him?

Not that she'd read much of the one she'd picked up, but still, what she had read was disturbing.

He ordered "the usual." Marnie ordered a salad with grilled chicken, dressing on the side. She prepared herself for the kind of casual conversation two strangers might have.

He looked at her, grimaced, and asked, "Why are you here?"

Marnie pursed her lips. Maybe she pouted, a little. Did Clint have some kind of dementia? She answered, in a calm, low voice, "You invited me to lunch."

That got an almost-grin out of him. "I mean, what are you doing here in Mystic Springs. You told me a bit about it when we met at Harry's, but you didn't say much. Why here? Why now?"

"Oh." That was a relief. He might write nightmare inducing tales of horror, but he wasn't crazy. At least his memory seemed to be working. "It was just luck that brought me here, I guess." She didn't know if it was good luck or bad luck, but it had been a strange series of circumstances. "Like I said before, I lost my job. Not because I did anything wrong, but you know how it is. Things happen. In this case, budget cuts. Soon after I was laid off, I ran across an online ad for a librarian here. Since Mystic Springs is fairly close to Birmingham and I needed the job, I decided to give it a try." The money was better than she'd expected from a small-town library, but she certainly wasn't going to complain about that.

Eve herself dropped off their plates. Marnie's salad looked

perfect. Clint's plate was piled high with steak and fish, with a side of fat yeast rolls. Four of them.

She was distracted, for a moment. "You don't eat vegetables?" At all?

"I get plenty of greens, but not when I eat at Eve's."

Clint took a bite, then another, while Marnie ended up thinking about the series of events that had brought her here. His question had brought those circumstances to the surface again. She'd gone back to the job-search website after she'd sent in her resume for another look at the want ad. She'd searched for a while, following link after link after link, but she hadn't been able to find it, even though the ad had popped out at her so clearly the first time around. She dribbled a small amount of dressing over her salad. Was that suspicious? Not really, though it was odd. She'd had more than her fair share of odd, lately.

She took a bite of her salad and instantly dismissed her misgivings. Holy cow, this was the best salad she'd ever eaten. Everything was so fresh, and the seasonings were perfect. Normally a salad was her "I've eaten badly so now I need to be good" meal, but this one was a real treat.

Marnie knew what she'd be eating for a while. Eve's salads and Ivy's goodies. A balanced diet! Maybe one day she'd actually get a cupcake like the one painted on Ivy's window.

There was no conversation while they ate. At least, not for a while. If Clint's meal was as good as hers, it was no wonder they enjoyed a shared and easy silence.

Finally, Marnie set her fork aside and leaned back, completely satisfied. "Eve should open a place in Birmingham. She could make a small fortune. If she'd share her recipes, she could start a chain of restaurants."

Clint shook his head. "It'll never happen. She's a Springer, through and through."

"A Springer?"

"A native of Mystic Springs. She was born here, and she'll never leave."

That was odd. People, especially those of Eve's age, were usually eager to escape small town living. Marnie certainly had been, and so had all her high school friends.

"Never?"

Clint caught and held her gaze, and a shiver walked up Marnie's spine. Oh, those blue eyes! They were electric. Mesmerizing. Sexy as hell. He shook his head.

"What about you?"

He shrugged his shoulders and returned his attention to what was left on his plate. "I travel now and then, but I always come back home."

"Where have you traveled?"

He thought a moment, then said, "Florida, a couple of times. A little town north of Dallas. North Georgia. The South Carolina coast."

Marnie smiled. "You never leave the South?"

He shrugged. "The cold doesn't agree with me."

She could empathize. "After I graduated from college I worked in Minneapolis for a while," she said. "One winter was enough for me."

"Where's home?"

"Tennessee, west of Nashville." In what she'd once believed to be a small town, until she'd come here.

Clint looked like he was about to ask another question, probably wanting more specifics which she would not be eager to share, when something drew his attention. His gaze shifted, settling on something behind her. Curious, Marnie turned a bit and twisted her head to look out the front window.

A dark-haired man in khaki shorts and a matching shirt ran down the middle of the street, chasing what looked to be a pack of wild dogs while he waved a long stick in the air. He shouted something unintelligible before he, and the dogs, disappeared from view.

Clint returned to his meal, what little was left of it. Marnie just stared at him for a moment, until he lifted his gaze to her and said, "That's Silas, the dogcatcher."

"The dogcatcher."

"He prefers Animal Control Specialist, but yeah. Dogcatcher." Clint seemed to bristle, a little. "Silas is also a Veterinarian, but since the town is too small to need both, he does double duty. Most just call him the critter guy."

"That's kind of rude."

He looked at her as if he were judging her, for some reason. "I suppose it is. He's pretty good with most critters, but not with that bunch." Clint smiled a little.

A few more customers had come in for lunch, so Marnie didn't feel quite as much on display as she had when they'd first arrived. Everyone was busy with their own meals, their own conversations. She took a casual glance around. The people here appeared normal enough, for the most part, though that one woman's hat was decidedly eye-catching, it was so wide and bright. It looked as if a peacock had perched upon her head.

It wasn't long before she heard the same noise that had distracted her a couple of minutes earlier and saw Silas, the critter guy, retracing his steps. Somehow the dogs – there were six of them, she noted this time, a mix in color and size -- had gotten around him and he was herding them back the way they'd come.

Silas glanced toward Eve's, slowed his step a bit, smiled, and waved. Marnie couldn't tell exactly who he was waving at; if that raised hand was meant for a specific person or if it was a general gesture because he knew people had to be watching.

And then he was out of sight, and all the diners returned to their meals as if nothing had happened. As if it was normal to see the town vet/dogcatcher chasing a pack of dogs down the middle of Main Street.

She picked at what was left of her salad. "Tell me about the previous librarian. I hear she was elderly and that she passed away a few weeks ago, but that's all I know." She also knew that the woman had not died in the library. For some reason, that eased her mind. Not that she believed in ghosts, or anything, but she was kind of a believer in energy, and if anything could bring bad energy to a place it was an unpleasant death. And was any death *pleasant*?

Clint made a low noise that was just short of a grunt. "Alice Daniels was librarian here for as long as I can remember. She was tough and demanded silence in her library from everyone at all times, and I swear she knew exactly where every book in that place was located."

"You liked her, I can tell."

"I did."

That was a point in his favor, that he'd had tender feelings for the elderly librarian. Of course, he had to love books, too, given his chosen profession. "Susan said she died at home. That's so sad. Had she been sick or was her death sudden?"

Clint frowned at her. His eyes narrowed. A muscle in his jaw ticked. "Susan didn't tell you?"

Marnie's heart sank. She didn't like the sound of this! "Didn't tell me what?"

He didn't answer immediately, but did his best to stare right through her with those electric-blue eyes of his. Marnie's heart tried to climb into her throat, but she managed to choke it back. Suddenly, she didn't want to hear what he had to say.

And then he said it. "Alice Daniels was murdered."

Clint watched as the blood drained from Marnie's face. Maybe he should've beat around the bush a while, shared the news gently.

Gentle was not his style.

He shouldn't have said anything at all. The town council and the police chief had gone to great lengths to hide the truth from everyone outside Mystic Springs, as well as most residents. They didn't need investigators from the county or the state coming in to poke around. Any investigation would have to be entirely local. Two months in, and they had nothing. He should have kept his mouth shut.

"I have to be getting back," Marnie said, tossing her napkin to the table and sliding across her seat so she could escape. "Thanks for lunch."

She was going to run. She was going to flee from this strange place as soon as she possibly could. Murdered librarians. Unfriendly locals. Critter man on the loose. Bigfoot.

Some Springers would be glad to see her go, but Clint decided then and there that he would not be one of those people.

He liked her.

Luke said the town needed her.

Maybe he did, too.

Shit. He barely knew her, and he'd been sitting here watching her every move as casually as he possibly could. She was pretty, very pretty, but her appeal went beyond that. Marnie was bright and feminine and curious. There were moments when he could swear she actually glowed. Her shape was fantastic, with generous curves in all the right places. Even the dark rimmed eyeglasses suited her.

Maybe he seriously needed to get laid. It had been a while.

"It was a tragedy," he said, "but they caught the man who killed Alice." He shared the story they'd told to all those who didn't know the truth of what had happened to the old librarian. They would've told everyone she'd died of natural causes, if she hadn't so obviously died violently, and if Mike Benedict's wife

Cindy hadn't been the one to find the body. Cindy had a lot of good qualities. Keeping her mouth shut wasn't one of them. "The killer was a drugged-up drifter who was obviously after her cash and jewelry, even though she didn't have much of either. I guess he thought an old woman who lived alone would be an easy target. He was wrong. Alice fought back and the drifter ran, but she bled to death before she could get to a phone to call for help. Her attacker was found in the woods less than a mile away, dead from the knife wound she managed to inflict."

Marnie was still pale, perched on the edge of her seat poised to run, likely wondering what she was doing in this place. "How could an old woman possibly fight back against someone like that?"

She was a witch wouldn't go over well, so he fudged a little. "Alice was a fighter. She was tough as nails." *And she looked pretty good for 127 years old.*

Marnie sighed. "You don't expect to hear stories like that in a place like this. Small towns are supposed to be safe. Elderly librarians aren't supposed to be robbed and murdered."

"There's darkness everywhere."

Marnie almost smiled. Almost. Her lips twisted a bit, but her eyes... those great, dark eyes didn't hold even a hint of a smile. "Spoken like a horror novelist." She sighed. "I have to get back. It's been thirty-five minutes and I said I'd be gone half an hour. Not that anyone would notice. No one comes into the library. No one! It's just not natural." With that she stood, brushing off her skirt. Damn, she had a great figure. She was a little short, maybe, but then again every woman and the majority of men in town were shorter than he was.

He was supposed to keep an eye on her until it was decided if it was safe to let her stay. As he watched her walk away, Clint decided that the hardcore Springers who were determined to run Marnie out of town would have to come through him if they wanted to hurt her or try to force her to leave.

Was she safe here? Could he keep her safe until he decided whether or not he needed her as much as it felt like he did at this moment?

At least she'd bought the story about Alice's death. The truth was, they had no idea who'd murdered the old woman. Or why. Now was not the time to tell Marnie that the old witch had been killed in the house she was currently living in.

CHAPTER 7

MARNIE RETURNED to the front desk and took a seat. For once, she was glad of the solitude. Clint was a stud, but he was really not her type. She preferred a gentler sort of man. Clint was smart, he was handsome — in a rough and rugged kind of way — but he wasn't refined. He was blunt and strong and *big*. He'd be great in a crisis, she imagined, this tough guy, but big and tough had never been on her list of the attributes she wanted in a man. She'd settled for Jay. Next time around, there would be no settling.

She wanted it all. Refinement, intelligence, looks, a sense of humor, and great sex. That wasn't too much to ask, was it? Both her parents were failures at marriage. Neither of them seemed to be able to choose wisely. Her brother had done okay with his wife of almost ten years. If he could break the mold, so could she.

Needing the distraction after hearing about what had happened to the previous librarian, she returned to her Bigfoot research. She moved on to the newest of the non-fiction books on the subject and flipped to the back cover.

Judging by the photo, which for all she knew might be twenty years old, the author was under forty years old and so handsome he qualified as pretty. His dark hair was too long, and waved as if it had been styled. His eyes were intelligent, his clothing casual but, to her eye, expensive.

Not that any of the authors she'd met actually looked like their publicity photos. Except Clint.

Nelson Lovell traveled the world searching for Bigfoot. He was a renowned cryptozoologist from Oregon, according to his bio, where apparently there had been many Bigfoot sightings. He'd caught a glimpse of one on a camping trip when he'd been twelve years old, and had been searching for proof ever since. She could sympathize with his obsession.

Marnie started reading and decided almost immediately that she enjoyed Lovell's writing style. It was smooth, easy, captivating, with a hint of humor and a handful of what her dad called two-dollar words. *Lovell* wouldn't give her nightmares.

She was at the start of chapter three when the door opened. Accustomed to being alone, she jumped a little at the sound of the chime.

A young woman with a baby on her hip walked into the library. The woman smiled. Smiled! The baby squirmed and squealed, and the smile dimmed a little. "Clint said you might be able to help me. I'm looking for something to help with a baby who refuses to sleep. I tried looking on the internet, but it was maddening. There's too much information and I don't know what to believe."

Marnie set the Lovell book aside and stood, giving the young woman her own smile. "I know exactly what you mean. I have just the book for you."

She walked confidently toward the non-fiction section. She'd had a couple of days to acquaint herself with the layout, so she didn't falter. No one trusted a librarian who didn't know her way around the stacks of books. How lame would that be? Marnie introduced herself as they walked, and the young woman did the same. Her name was Gabi Lawson, and she had a booth at the hair salon down the street. Of course she was a hair stylist! Gabi's mid-length hair, which was almost as dark as Marnie's, looked like something out of a shampoo commercial. Thick, wavy, shiny, well-behaved...

No photoshopping required.

Gabi's beautiful baby was named Mia, an appropriately pretty name for the blue-eyed mostly bald girl.

Marnie easily located the book she had in mind, one that several mothers at the Birmingham library had sworn by, and then she helped Gabi look through a few other books, some old and some new. As she searched, she found her mind wandering. She hated it when that happened.

She'd taken to calling the unwanted thoughts that popped up when she least expected them *memory turds*. They normally came at night, when she wanted to sleep but could not, but now and then they came during the daytime, when she should be concentrating on whatever she was doing at that moment. Instead of thinking of books for the new mother, she remembered what Clint had said about the old librarian being murdered.

That memory would not go away. It probably never would. Marnie hadn't given up on her Bigfoot research, but now she had a murder to look into, as well. She'd taken Clint's word about what had happened, but the more she thought about it the less certain she was that he'd been entirely honest. A drugged-up drifter, here? One did not simply run across Mystic Springs. If a drifter had wandered off the main road — if it could be called "main" in any way — would he have kept going until he made it all the way in? She remembered her trip into town all too well. It seemed unlikely that anyone would stumble across the place, but she supposed it wasn't impossible.

Why hadn't Susan shared the all-important tidbit that the previous librarian had been murdered? She hadn't lied, exactly. Alice Daniels hadn't been a young woman, and she had passed away at home. All true. Susan just hadn't shared the news that the old woman had been helped along in her exit from this world.

Bigfoot. Murder. The best food she'd ever tasted, a fantastic library… and some of the oddest people she'd ever met.

And Clint. She hadn't decided yet which category to put him in. Was he an asset or a distraction? A reason to stay or a reason to go? It didn't really matter. She had no intention of getting involved with anyone at the moment, much less a man who ate like a horse and wrote about monsters, about blood and guts. She'd tried to use logic to convince herself that Clint was not for her, but sometimes logic didn't work as it should. There was something about him…

She made her decision as she walked Gabi to the front desk, trying once more to call on cold reason. Blue eyes and great body aside, Clint Maxwell was a distraction she did not need or want.

———

I've seen Bigfoot. What do I do?

Have you seen or heard of Bigfoot in Alabama? Let me tell you…

Help!

Sitting at one of the computers in the back of the library, Marnie pondered what she might say in her email to Nelson Lovell. She started a message to him four times, each time backspacing in frustration to delete every word she'd written. Eventually she cancelled the message entirely. What she needed was proof. A picture, maybe. Definitely a picture. She'd seen the creature twice. Surely she would see him again. This time she'd be ready, phone in hand.

Librarian discovers proof of mythical monster. She'd be famous.

She didn't really want to be famous. Rich? Yes. Famous seemed to be more hassle than it was worth.

Marnie cleared the history on the public computer — given how infrequently it was used she didn't know why she bothered, but it was the thing to do — and returned to the front desk. She put away the Lovell book, half finished, and picked up Clint's novel. She knew him, so she really should actually read at least one of his books all the way through. A slick yellow bookmark advertising the Mystic Springs Public Library marked the last page she'd read.

He'd sent her a real live person looking for assistance, so she'd repay the favor by reading his book. She steeled her spine for more bloodcurdling violence, and she got it.

For a chapter or two. After a couple of truly savage scenes, she reached a chapter that had been written from the monster's point of view. There was heartbreaking sadness in this beast's heart. He didn't want to kill, didn't want to be feared and loathed. It reminded her a little of the old movies where the monsters, most of them anyway, didn't want to be monsters. They didn't want to kill, they were driven by something deeper and darker than they could understand.

She began to feel sympathy for the possessor of the claws. Her heart broke for him.

Damn. Clint could write!

She set the book aside and wiped away an unexpected tear. It was a surprise to see how much time had passed since she'd gotten back to it. The afternoon had flown by, and she hadn't done a bit of research on the death of the previous librarian. Maybe it was too late to start.

The man who had murdered the old woman was a real monster, one she could never feel sympathy for. The details of that death would give her horrendous nightmares. She supposed she could look into the death on her own computer, at home, but then again, she much preferred fiction to reality, and researching murder close to bedtime was probably not a good idea. Tomorrow would be soon enough to investigate that crime.

It was almost time to lock up and head home when she went back to the computer and composed an email.

Dear Mr. Lovell,
I've found Bigfoot.

"What was I supposed to do, not tell her?" Clint shouted.

Someone had overheard his conversation with Marnie over lunch, and that someone had gone directly to Susan.

"That's exactly what you should have done. If she gets curious…"

"She won't."

"Do you really believe that?"

"If she finds even a hint of the truth, she won't believe it."

Sitting in the cushy chair by the window, Susan squirmed a little and gave a long-suffering sigh, as she settled in. She glanced out the window, onto a wooded view she might've normally found soothing. Nothing could truly soothe him, or Susan, at the moment.

"If she asks the wrong person the wrong questions we'll have no choice but to get her out of town," Susan said. "One way or another. If that happens, I won't be able to bring in an outsider again. We need new blood, Clint. There are a handful of Non-Springers in town, but not nearly enough."

"Maybe we should take it slow," he suggested.

She looked at him then. "We can't take it slow." Some might call Susan a witch — goodness knows Mystic Springs had more than its share — though she was not nearly as powerful as Alice had been. Like Luke, she sometimes just knew things. Susan was easy-going, and people liked her. Maybe that was part of her gift; he didn't know for sure, but she was — and had always been — a steadying influence on the town.

Something was eating at Susan. She wasn't her normal, easy-going self. "The town doesn't have much time," she said. "If it isn't revitalized, it's going to die. Not slowly, not in a matter of years, but with a bang. What will happen to us then? You know what it's like away from town, away from the springs. The magic dies. Who we are fades, until there's nothing left. There might be times when we wish to be ordinary, but we aren't, and we will never be."

He didn't wish to be ordinary, and neither did Susan. Any Springer who did had only to walk away, and soon enough their wish would come true.

Hundreds of years ago — no one knew exactly how many hundreds — a powerful witch had cast a spell over Mystic Springs. As far as they could tell, the result was almost like a bubble or a dome. Within the bubble, their abilities flourished. Outside of it for any length of time weakened them, and eventually completely muted their powers. Everyone was different, in how they handled being away from Mystic Springs for more than a few days.

He didn't dare stay away for more than a couple of weeks at a time.

"Didn't you spend a couple of years in Atlanta?" he asked.

"I did," Susan looked at him. Her usual air of tranquility was fractured, disturbed. "It was horrible. I felt incomplete, as surely as if I'd lost an arm or a leg, my sight or my hearing. I wasn't... me."

Springers had tried for years to address the problem of population decline. Unfortunately, it was difficult to find more than half a dozen people who agreed on the solution. Some wanted to remove the shield entirely, which would allow them to go out into the world with their magical abilities intact. It would also allow the powers of those who'd left Mystic Springs, even those who might unknowingly have Springer blood, to awaken.

The opposite plan would be even more drastic. Brigadoon. If the shield was strengthened the town would disappear, be erased from the outside world. No one would come in; no one would be able to leave.

So far no one had figured out how to do either, though for years many had tried. Alice among them.

Clint was among those who preferred the status quo, imperfect as it was.

"I don't have any answers, but I agree, we can't continue to be isolated from the outside world." Too many Springers had left. Maybe they'd been glad to become normal, after a while. Given the way their population had dwindled, a lot of Springers had been happy to embrace whatever change being out of the bubble brought them.

"You like her, don't you?" Susan asked with a gentle smile.

He didn't have to ask who she was talking about. "I don't like anyone," he said, perhaps a bit too defensively.

Susan's smile didn't last. "She will need you to protect her, if she's going to stay."

"Yeah. I know."

Clint stared at the councilwoman, his friend, a distant cousin — as so many of the Springers were. "It's bad enough that you've got her living right next door to…"

"She loves the house, and I don't think she's met any of her neighbors. She's not likely to, not anytime soon. You know how they are. It'll be fine."

Fine. Nothing was fine, but he didn't bother to argue the point.

"And couldn't you have put her in another house? If she finds out…"

"If she finds out and is displeased, we'll find her another place to live. Alice's place was move-in ready. Most of the others need some work."

As houses did, when they were neglected.

"I don't think she'll be displeased. I think she'll freak out."

"Well then, I guess we'd better make sure she doesn't find out."

There was no immediate response from Nelson Lovell, but then Marnie hadn't really expected one. He might not check his email every day, or he might be in the middle of the woods, anywhere in the world, setting up cameras and hoping, as she had, for a photograph to prove what he believed – what he *knew* – to be true. According to his book he traveled a lot, exploring this country and others in search of Bigfoot.

Then again, he might have an assistant who deleted all the crazy messages that came in. Her message might've been deleted after a glance.

She needed a picture.

Her navy skirt had a pocket, so she chose it for the day, along with a white blouse and her red shoes. She loved red shoes, and these heels were her favorites. Her cell phone went into the pocket. It would be close at all times, even though she didn't expect to see Bigfoot in the library.

As had become her habit, she walked to work. This morning, her neighbor to the east was sitting on his front porch. Marnie waved as she walked down her own porch steps. The old man rocked once, then turned his head and looked at her, but did not return her greeting. She was horrified to realize that her neighbor was the one who'd glared at her so hatefully just yesterday, in Eve's place. She would not be borrowing a cup of sugar — or whatever else neighbors borrowed from one another — from him, she imagined.

She had other things on her mind this morning, and quickly put the surly neighbor from her mind. The library closed at noon on Thursday and Saturday. Sunday was her only full day off, but the two half days made up for that. After lunch she'd put on her running shoes and explore the land between the rear of the library and the river. Maybe she'd work her way over to the woods behind her house. There were plenty of places for creatures to hide there.

Not after dark, though. She wouldn't be able to get a good

picture after dark. Yeah, *that* was the reason she intended to be inside with the doors locked behind her when darkness fell.

Instead of her usual oatmeal, muffins from Ivy's, along with a big cup of coffee, had served as breakfast. Ivy, while not so pleasant, was as talented as her sister in the kitchen. They must've grown up in a household where they learned how to cook, and to do it well. Marnie's own mother, bless her heart, was great with take-out and could put together a fantastic lasagna, but beyond that she wasn't much of a cook. One of the stepmothers who'd been around during Marnie's teenage years had been a great cook, but she hadn't lasted long enough to teach her unhappy stepdaughter anything. Marnie wondered if Eve and Ivy gave lessons. Would they share their culinary secrets? A cooking school! That would be perfect. She'd attend the Mystic Springs Culinary Academy in a heartbeat.

If she got the chance. She'd only been in town a few days, but it was looking less and less like she'd stay for any length of time. The library was fantastic, except for the lack of users. The town was charming, if you discounted the "don't go out after dark" warning, the murder of the last librarian, and the glares she got from far too many of the locals. "Charming" would only balance out so much.

Then there was Clint, the hot local horror writer. He got under her skin in a big way, but he wasn't what she was looking for in the romance department. Not at all. So why did he make her so damned antsy? No man who purposely gave her nightmares should make her squirm in a not entirely unpleasant way.

And of course she couldn't forget Bigfoot. The two sightings had been horrifying and fascinating, exciting and terrifying. She wanted a picture before she left.

But first things first.

Marnie sat down at the computer in the middle of the trio at the back desk. The chairs there were not at all comfortable, and she had to adjust the one she was in a couple of times to make it tolerable. Unlike yesterday, she planned to sit here for a while. Once she was settled in, she went to the internet and typed *Alice Daniels* into the search bar. It wasn't an entirely uncommon name, so she had to sift through a large number of unrelated links. You'd think an article about a recent murder would come up near the top. It should at the very least make it to a spot on the first ten pages.

She found absolutely nothing. Not even a mention in the Eufaula newspaper. There wasn't even an obituary, not that she could find.

Wasn't the murder of a librarian bigger news than this? Marnie certainly thought it should be.

Sitting in the back corner, facing an uncooperative computer and a plain white wall, Marnie suddenly felt vulnerable. She'd never worried about being alone in this library or any other, but at this moment a warning tingle walked up her spine. The hairs on the back of her neck stood up. She would've heard the chime if someone had come into the library, and there had been none. Still, she was almost positive that someone was watching her.

Not a friendly someone, either. Marnie turned her head slowly, certain someone would be there. Someone watching. Someone lurking. People who didn't intend to do harm didn't lurk!

She swiveled in her chair; she scanned what she could see of the library, the shelves of books, the narrow aisles. She saw nothing, nothing at all, but the feeling that she was being watched didn't abate. After a moment, she stood and walked away from the computer station, taking one aisle and then another in her return to the front desk, peering around corners and over the tops of books to catch a glimpse of another aisle. Just reading about the murder had her imagination working overtime. If someone had come in she would've heard the sound announcing the arrival of a visitor. She'd been near the rear door, which locked up tight, and would've seen anyone coming in that way. The front door, complete with chime, was the only other way in.

She'd almost convinced herself that the feeling of being watched had been a weird reaction to lack of information about Alice Daniels' murder when she reached the desk and saw the note there, sitting smack dab in the middle of her work area.

Written in purple marker on a plain white sheet of paper, the tall words filled the page.

GO HOME.

The front door definitely chimed when she pushed her way through it.

Clint drove his pickup instead of walking into town, since there wasn't a moment to spare. According to Travis Benedict — Police Chief and older brother to Luke — there was no real emergency. Just a hysterical librarian. He considered a hysterical librarian a real emergency, especially if that librarian was Marnie.

The police station was small. Even when the town had been much healthier than it was these days, crime hadn't been much of an issue. It was tough to get away with much of anything in a town filled with telepaths, witches, and the occasional wizard.

Travis came from a long line of telepaths. Luke's ability was specific. He knew what you'd need before you did. The family gift seemed to have skipped Travis entirely. He was a Springer, had been born here, but he was one of the few who apparently possessed no supernatural abilities. Mike, the younger Benedict brother, had just a touch of the gift. Enough to be useful, but not so much that it affected his life negatively. He'd married a Non-Springer a couple years back. Amazingly enough, Cindy accepted this weird town and the weirder people in it. She loved her husband that much.

Travis was a good cop, but he still couldn't explain what had happened to Alice. Unfortunately, neither could anyone else in town, which made this a whole new kind of mystery. When none of the town psychics could solve a crime, there was definitely dark magic at work.

Magic flowed through Mystic Springs, and through the blood of the Springers. The gifts they'd been given might be weak or powerful, useful or amusing. Some abilities were specific and limited, while others seemed to grow and change over time.

Dark magic had the ability to hide.

Clint parked across the street from the police station, in front of the ice cream shop. He saw the owner of the shop, Jordan, on the other side of the glass, and gave her a distracted wave before turning to cross the street. When he walked through the police station door, Marnie jumped from her chair and sprinted toward him. She threw herself at him, launching herself through the air. He caught her.

Her heart pounded. Her breath came heavy. She clung to him, fitting against him in a way that felt disturbingly right and natural. She held on as if her life depended on it. Instinctively Clint turned his head so he could smell her better. He inhaled, slowly and deeply, and her scent filled him. A primitive instinct screamed *mine*.

It was fast, it was unexpected, and yet he had the feeling they'd been hurtling toward this moment since she'd seen him on the road, on her way into town. She'd been coming to him all along, she just hadn't realized it.

The possessive wave came and went quickly, but it was strong enough to freeze him in place for a long moment. What the hell had come over him? Marnie wasn't his and never would be.

"There was no chime, I swear it," she said breathlessly, without loosening her grip. "I was in the back, and I was busy, but I would've heard it. How did he get in? Why leave that… that note?"

Before Clint could ask "what note?" Travis lifted an evidence bag with a single, badly wrinkled sheet of paper in it. He could read the words from his position by the door.

Some asshole had disobeyed the council and was trying to scare Marnie out of town. Why?

Her body relaxed a little, and she gradually loosened her hold on him. He didn't want to let her go, he wanted to keep her close a while longer, but he did loosen his grip and allow her to slide down, slowly but surely. With her feet firmly planted on the ground once again, she trembled as she explained what had happened. He wanted to hold her again, to comfort her. But he didn't. He didn't dare.

Travis tried to suggest that Marnie had been so engrossed in whatever had been on the computer that she'd simply missed the sound at the front entrance. Her answer was a censuring, librarian-like glare.

"Being on the computer didn't deafen me, and I was hardly *engrossed*."

Travis shrugged, a dismissive gesture Marnie did not take well.

"What were you doing on the computer, anyway?" Clint asked. "Ordering new books for the library? Looking for a new job…"

She looked down and away, then back to him. "I wanted to see what kind of news was out there about the murder of the previous librarian."

"I told you…"

"Yes, I know, it was a drifter." She crossed her arms over her chest. "I don't quite buy that. There has to be more to the story. A drifter found his way into town and to Alice Daniels' house? I drove the road to get here. It's scary as hell. No one is going to *drift* into Mystic Springs, all the way through town, to a particular house."

Travis's face remained expressionless as he said, "Obviously he wasn't in his right mind."

For a long moment, Marnie stood there without speaking. Then she turned slowly, presenting her back to the chief and looking up at Clint. "Have you ever seen those scary movies where the characters make completely illogical decisions? They continue on long after any reasonable person would've gotten out. They *should* get out before things get completely hairy, it's only logical, but they never do."

Hairy. Interesting word choice...

He tried to present a logical argument. "You're talking about movies. Fiction. There would be no story if..."

Marnie ignored him and pointed a finger at her chest, poking herself squarely between two very fine breasts. "I am a reasonable person. If I hear a noise in the basement, I don't go into the basement. If a librarian is murdered and then I get a creepy note ordering me to get out, I'm going to get out."

She brushed past him, heading for the door.

He should let her go. Luke said the town needed her, and so did Susan, but there were other normals out there who could be brought in for the new blood the town so desperately needed. It didn't have to be her.

It didn't have to be her.

But he remembered the way she smelled, the way his body hummed when she was near, the way she sometimes glowed, for him and him alone. He also remembered his promise to himself that if anyone was going to run Marnie out of town, it was going to be him.

Before he spun on his heel, Travis said, "Let her go."

Maybe the police chief had a touch of the Benedict gift after all.

CHAPTER 8

Marnie walked down the sidewalk with purpose, eyes focused straight ahead. She didn't look at window displays, and she barely checked for oncoming cars when she crossed side streets. She could spend a couple of weeks, maybe a month, max, with her dad and stepmom number four. Stepmom wouldn't be happy, but her brother had no room, and her mom... well, her mom lived too far away and they hadn't had any kind of a close relationship for years.

That left her dad. She wouldn't have to live there for an extended period of time, just long enough to find another job. There were other jobs available, many of them, and she did have some savings. Not enough to throw away a perfectly good position at a great library, but still, she was smart, she was capable...

She was scared.

Marnie realized Clint was behind her long before he spoke. She felt him, as surely as if he'd placed a hand on her shoulder or at the small of her back. He had a presence; he disturbed the molecules in the air. At least, he disturbed the molecules in the air that surrounded her. She was always, *always*, aware of him.

Another reason to leave town ASAP.

"It was a harmless prank, I'm sure," he said as he drew up beside her.

She snorted.

"You're not going to let one note scare you out of town, are you?" His tone was almost teasing, but she was in no mood for a light-hearted jest.

"You bet your ass I am."

"Come on..."

She crossed the street and angled toward the library. At the door, she stopped.

Crap. In a horror movie she'd be the first to go! "I didn't lock the door," she whispered. "I ran out with that note clutched in my hand and headed straight for the police station. I didn't think about fingerprints or DNA on the paper, and I didn't lock the damn door." She turned her head and looked up at Clint. "I'm an idiot."

Anyone could be in there. Drifters. Note-writers. Librarian murderers.

Clint stepped past her and opened the door. "I'll take a look around."

He remained calm as he walked into the library. The door chimed, as it should. Naturally. Why hadn't it made that sound when the intruder had come in? The chime might be faulty. Even though she'd denied the possibility at the police station, she might've been so engrossed in her research that she'd simply not heard it. Somehow she didn't think either of those things were true.

She followed Clint, stopping just past the door to watch him search the main room of the library, then staying close as he moved further into the building. He was thorough, walking to the back of the room, checking to make sure the back door was locked, searching both bathrooms. Now and then he disappeared from her view for a few seconds, but never for long. A part of her stayed on edge, as she waited for someone, or something, to jump out of nowhere and surprise them both. Goodness knows there were plenty of places to hide.

Clint searched them all. After a while she relaxed, as he proved to her that no one was lurking around the next corner.

He stopped at the end of the staircase that led to the storeroom/break room and pointed up, as he lifted his eyebrows in question.

"I never lock that door," she said. Why on earth would she?

Clint walked up the stairs, and she followed. Was it wrong that she was distracted, again, by the way his butt filled those jeans? Of course it was wrong, and still, how could she not be? He had really good arms, too, muscled and tanned and, as she had initially judged, lumberjacky.

He opened the door and stepped inside. The room was small. It didn't take long for him to check the closets and then step into the bathroom for a look. There were literally no other places to hide.

"All well," he said as he exited the bathroom.

Marnie breathed a sigh of relief. She still intended to leave Mystic Springs soon, very soon, but at least she'd be able to sleep tonight. Maybe. Tomorrow she'd be gone. Normally she'd feel obligated to give two weeks' notice, but since no one came into the library, what difference did it make?

All she could do was nod at Clint, accepting his assurances.

Instead of passing her and exiting the room he walked directly to her. He stopped when he was, oh, maybe an inch or so away. She had always been aware of him, but so close, so wonderfully and terrifyingly close, it was as if she tingled from head to toe.

He dipped his head, and she looked up. She couldn't breathe. Her heart pounded so hard she was sure he could hear it. How could he not? A wise woman would back away. One step. Maybe two. She was apparently not so wise, not where Clint was concerned.

He looked into her eyes and whispered, "Don't leave. Give us a chance."

Us? Us as in the town, or us as in... *us*?

Was there an us?

She saw the kiss coming. Clint moved slowly, bringing his mouth toward hers. Now, while she was terrified? Did he think a kiss would calm her?

That was unlikely. Nothing about Clint soothed her. A simple look had the power to agitate her to the bone. A kiss? No, it would not calm her.

Marnie didn't move away, even though Clint was moving so slowly she had plenty of time to do so. She felt his body heat and inhaled his scent, which was clean and grassy and real. He was tall, really tall, but that didn't seem to matter as he leaned down and closer. Closer. Oh my God, he was *so close*.

They could make it work. She had never wanted anything as badly as she wanted him to kiss her. Her eyes closed and her lips parted a half second before his arrived.

It was an easy kiss, and definitely not her first. And yet, it was unlike any other she had ever experienced. She felt that kiss through her entire body. Two seconds in, she knew that if Clint asked her to sleep with him she wouldn't even hesitate, even though in horror movies sex was a sure step toward violent death. She lifted her right hand and grabbed the front of his shirt. One of his very fine arms wrapped around her and tightened, just a little. In his arms she was safe, warm, and incredibly turned on. She didn't want the kiss to end.

She couldn't kiss him long enough, deep enough. He growled a little. A soft sound of what had to be something akin to desperation formed in her throat and then escaped. Hadn't she said time and again that he wasn't her type? Her body did not agree.

The kiss ended, as it had to, but they didn't move apart. She didn't release his shirt, and he didn't drop his arm.

"Are you trying to convince me to stay?"

"What if I am?" His voice was wonderfully husky; his blue eyes were hooded. A lock of hair had fallen over his forehead, and she itched to push it back.

"I can't be so shallow."

"Why not?"

Why not, indeed? She lifted her hand to right the lock of hair that had caught her attention, but never got to scratch that particular itch.

The door to the storeroom stood open, so she clearly heard the door chime. She jumped back, her heart pounded — and not in a pleasant way.

So much for magic...

Clint walked down the stairs ahead of Marnie, in case someone was attempting to leave another nasty note. Or something worse. He wasn't entirely surprised to see Susan standing by the front desk. When she saw him her concerned expression was transformed, and she smiled.

She looked far too amused.

"I heard about the excitement and decided to check on you," she said, looking past him to Marnie.

"News travels fast," he said.

"Travis called me," Susan responded. "He was concerned."

"He didn't seem very concerned while I was there," Marnie complained, almost but not quite beneath her breath.

"Oh, dear." Susan walked past him to take Marnie's hand. "Don't be fooled by the casual air of our chief. That's just Travis's way." She tsked. "I can tell you're upset. Your face is still flushed, and..." She stopped abruptly, looked at Marnie a moment longer, and then turned her head to study Clint for a long moment before returning her attention to Marnie. There were few secrets in a town like this one. "In any case, please be assured that the

Mystic Springs Police Force takes your case very seriously and will find the culprit."

The Mystic Springs Police Force sounded impressive, unless you knew that it consisted of Chief Travis Benedict, and Travis alone.

A few minutes ago Marnie had been intent on leaving. Not today, it was too late for her to get packed and arrange for a place to go, but by morning...

Was she about to quit? He hadn't kissed her in an attempt to get her to stay, but if it did the trick he would not complain.

He'd had sexual relationships after his divorce, but none had ever felt permanent. Women came and went. They had fun and in the end either he or she decided it was time to move on. He didn't blame those who had been the ones to break off the relationship. He held back so much of himself, knowing he could never be totally honest, knowing there could never be anything more than sex. He could not, would not share the truth about himself with a Non-Springer. And if he didn't share the truth of what he was, how could he have a relationship that went any further than sex?

With Springers, how could he ever know that any woman he formed a bond with wouldn't try to change him? With or without his permission. Jenna had tried, and he hadn't seen it coming. He'd been hurt and angry, and the truth was that kind of betrayal left a mark. He'd loved her. He had not been enough for her.

Love the man, love the beast. They were one and the same.

Just sex was fine with him. It had to be. None of his post-divorce relationships had taken place here in Mystic Springs. No, they happened when he was out of town, when he traveled for research... when he could pretend he was someone else...

He'd kissed Marnie once, and already it felt as if she could be permanent. She was different. Odd, scattered, smart, beautiful. But more than that he felt connected to her on a cellular level, as if he had instantly recognized her as being his. From the moment she'd seen him in Harry's. Perhaps before.

Had he recognized her from a distance? Was that why he'd stopped in the street and allowed her to get a good, long look at him in his Dyn Gwallt state? There weren't many strangers in town so it wasn't like he had to be careful. He was quick, and usually that was enough. He had not moved on quickly when he'd seen Marnie. If he had, if he had not gone to her house that night, and again the next day, she would have easily written off that fleeting glance.

He had all but dared her to recognize him, to really see him.

He'd never given much credence to the theory that when it came to shifters, there was a predetermined mate. A woman meant for every man. A man destined to claim that one woman. In the old days, maybe, but in the 21st century? How could that be?

But as he watched Marnie gather her strength to speak, he realized that if she left tomorrow morning, he'd be right behind her.

———

It was on the tip of her tongue to tell Susan that she was done. Thanks, but no thanks, bye-bye. Good luck. But over Susan's shoulder, there was Clint. Tall, muscled, handsome in a not-pretty way, not her type, unwanted distraction, kisses like an angel Clint.

In that moment it seemed silly to flee in fear over a note. She already knew some from Mystic Springs didn't like strangers — including Ivy Franklin — but it wasn't like the note had been written in blood, or anything. The ink had been purple, which was apparently Ivy's favorite color, but would the baker have been so obvious? She seemed smarter than that. Maybe it had just been a prank, as Clint had suggested. This town definitely had more than its share of odd people. Maybe she could give Mystic Springs, and this fabulous library, another chance.

Yes, it was true, she was allowing herself to be influenced by a single kiss.

There was a welcome reception planned for tomorrow evening, and it would be rude to leave before that took place. She couldn't be rude. Nannie, rest her soul, would be horrified. Marnie's earlier panic had faded, somewhat, and while she was not thrilled with the day's events, she wasn't ready to run either.

Had she been swayed by common sense or by that kiss? She really wanted to convince herself that she was calling on logic, not emotion, but it was a hard sell.

"Maybe I overreacted," she said in a lowered voice.

"Oh, I wouldn't say that," Susan said kindly.

"Neither would I," Clint added in a lowered voice. "Until Travis finds something, one way or another, I'll keep an eye on things here."

Susan smiled and glanced Clint's way. "Writer's block?"

He shrugged. "Could be."

Marnie squirmed. What did he mean by *keep an eye on things here*? From the outside? From inside? Exactly how close did he intend to be while he kept an eye on things?

At the moment, it didn't matter. She couldn't imagine that he'd ever be close enough.

Again, the chime over the front door sounded. Marnie jumped like she'd been shot.

The little girl she'd seen skipping down the street yesterday bounced into the library, a thin, hardback book clutched in one hand. "I know this book is overdue," the child said as she placed it on the front counter. "But I don't think I should have to pay a fine because the library was closed."

"Felicity Adams," Susan said in a censuring voice, "is that any way to introduce yourself to the new librarian? Now, give Miss Somerset a proper greeting."

The girl sighed. "How do you do, Miss Somerset. I'm Felicity Adams." She smiled widely. "I love the library so you will see me a lot, I'm afraid." With that she all but danced toward the back of the room. Oh, to have that kind of energy!

Clint, her own parlor, and a little girl who loved the library as much as Marnie had as a child. Yes, she could give this job, and this town, one more chance…

After Susan and Felicity left, Marnie locked the door. Susan had remained her normal serene and cheerful self, supremely unconcerned about the note or the malfunctioning door chime. Felicity had sauntered off with three young adult books tucked under her arm and a satisfied smile on her face.

The little girl reminded Marnie of how much she'd loved the library as a child. And as an adult. Maybe there was hope for Mystic Springs yet.

Maybe.

It was well past noon, the normal closing time for Thursday. There were several hours of daylight left, since the summer days were long, but she doubted she'd be taking any Bigfoot photos today. She was exhausted. Besides, she couldn't expect that she could just walk toward the woods and the thing would appear. It might take days, weeks, maybe months before she had an opportunity to take a picture. If she ever did.

She wouldn't be here for months. Weeks? Unlikely. Days, maybe.

Marnie didn't turn around for a moment. Clint stood behind her, and she wasn't quite ready to look him in the eye.

"I'm sure I'll be fine…" she began, turning slowly.

"I'm not," he said.

How could he be so calm? How could he act as if nothing had happened?

She wasn't talking about the note anymore.

She and Jay had been on four dates before they'd slept

together. They'd known each other much longer than that, and had been to a number of dinners and parties with mutual friends. She'd known him well, had been aware of his flaws and his assets. She really had thought they worked as a couple before they took that step. In the end it turned out she'd been kidding herself.

She barely knew Clint. So why was she so certain that if he stuck around to keep an eye on her, he'd end up in her bed? And would that be a *bad* thing?

Yes, it would.

Then again, maybe not.

"Take a deep breath," he said in a low, soothing voice. "You look like you're about to pass out."

That would be embarrassing.

"I just want to crawl into bed and get under the covers," she said, and then she clarified, too sharply, "For a nap! I'm exhausted."

"I understand."

Maybe he did, and maybe he didn't. It was likely he thought if he agreed with everything she said, she'd fall onto her back. She could be had, but she wasn't easy. "I don't handle abject terror very well."

Lord, he had a great smile. He flashed it for her now. "You need food."

"No, I need..." Her stomach growled, loudly. "Yes, I need food, but I think a sandwich and a glass of tea on my back porch is just what the doctor ordered." Clint had bought her dinner Monday night, and lunch just yesterday, so another meal at Eve's... would he consider that a third date? Some people said that third date was *the one*, and while she was in many ways ready and willing, she wasn't exactly sure...

He'd said yesterday's lunch was not a date, but still, best not to take any chances.

"I'll walk you home." It was an order, not a request, delivered as he took her arm to steady her. Yes, she needed to be steadied.

Marnie collected her purse and headed for the door, eager to get out of here. As she grabbed her bag from a shelf at the front desk, she had a passing thought that it, too, had been unguarded when some creep had left that warning note. And when she'd run to the police station. And while she and Clint had been upstairs and he'd been effectively kissing her senseless.

This was a great library, it was her library — for the moment — but dammit, she had been so scared to realize that while she'd thought she was alone someone had been watching.

She checked, just to be sure, and yes, the house key was there in a side pocket of her purse, right where she'd left it. Still, having an escort home wasn't such a bad idea. Especially if that escort was Clint Maxwell.

CHAPTER 9

THE COTTAGE SUSAN had assigned to Marnie was decent enough, he supposed, as long as you weren't disturbed by the fact that a woman had been murdered there. It was small, the kitchen appliances were out of date, and there was just one bathroom, as he recalled. Of course, there was a single person living there, so one bathroom was plenty.

If Marnie found out now that Alice had been murdered here, in this house, she'd be out of town before dark.

"This is me," she said as she turned down the walkway from the sidewalk. "Thanks for the escort."

Clint stopped, watching her walk on without looking back. Damn, she had a great ass, a sexy walk, a curvy shape that would drive any man to distraction. As she reached the front steps she came to a halt with one foot on the bottom step. She looked back, and those dark eyes seemed to bore right through him.

"Want me to check the house for you?" he asked, his voice low.

Judging by her expression, she had just this moment wondered if the person who'd found his way into the library might have also found his way into her home. The idea terrified her.

If he didn't do something, she wouldn't be here much longer. *Mystic Springs needs the librarian.* If those words were true...

"I guess," she said in a weak voice.

He tried to smile, to show her that he was confident no one had invaded her home. He wasn't sure, but he suspected Susan had put some kind of protection spell on the cottage. She had to know that not everyone would be glad to see a stranger come to town. Susan's magic wasn't the most powerful in town, not by a long shot, so any spell of that kind would only be partially effective.

They'd both feel better if he had a look around.

Marnie unlocked the front door then moved back; he stepped around her and walked into the house first. Everything seemed to be in place in the living room. The kitchen was neat, with one plate and one coffee cup sitting in the sink. As he had recalled, the appliances were ancient. Maybe she didn't cook much and didn't care. The spare bedroom at the front, just off the living room — the room where Alice had died — was equally tidy, with a few sealed cardboard boxes scattered about, among the partially unpacked boxes. There was no place to hide in the small dining room, but he gave it the once over as he walked through to the bathroom. There weren't many places to hide there, but he checked the clawfoot tub. Just in case.

He saved Marnie's bedroom for last.

The closet door stood open, and shoes were scattered everywhere. Clothes were tossed onto a small wingback chair and on the floor. The bed looked as if it had been not just slept in, but well used. Pillows on the floor, comforter tossed over the end, sheets askew.

"Damn, it looks like..."

Marnie skirted around him, eased him out of the room, and

closed the door. "I'm a restless sleeper, and this morning I couldn't decide what to wear."

Clint tipped his head and looked down at her. She was close, very close, having rushed in to shut the door on her messy bedroom. He should back up, at least a little bit, but he didn't. He liked having her close. He wanted to open that door, toss her onto the rumpled bed, and rumple it some more.

He didn't mean to growl, he really didn't...

Marnie's eyes widened. She ducked down and slipped past him once again, this time in order to escape.

He was too old to play games, and so was she. The attraction was mutual. It was strong. It was damn near undeniable. He followed her to the kitchen.

"It's going to happen, you know," he said. "We're going to sleep together." A nice way to put it. If he ever got her into that bed, there wasn't going to be a lot of sleeping going on.

Marnie opened the refrigerator and pulled out a pitcher of tea. She didn't say anything as she fetched two glasses from the cupboard. Two. That was good. She didn't intend to immediately push him out the door.

She sighed, and as she filled the glasses she said, "I don't want to rush into anything. We should take our time, get to know one another better, maybe go on a date."

"Technically we've been on two."

She looked at him. "Do they count? As I recall, you specifically said lunch was *not* a date."

"I did, didn't I?" Clint took the glass she handed him. "You want to be wooed."

"That's kind of an old-fashioned word for it, but I guess, yes. Woo me."

Flowers. Candy. Dancing? Shit, he did not dance. If he took her out to dinner it would have to be at Eve's or Harry's. Neither qualified as romantic. The whole town would be watching. Hell, he didn't do romantic. Not for anyone. At least, not for anyone else.

He placed his glass on the kitchen table, took hers from her hand and set it beside his, then wrapped his arms around her. "I'm going to kiss you again."

Her eyes were wide. "Okay." And then, before he could move toward her she rose up on her toes and kissed him. His surprise didn't last long.

It was a good kiss. Deep and mesmerizing, soft and powerful. They picked up right where they'd left off, when Susan had come into the library and interrupted them. He was driven; he didn't ever want to let Marnie go. Maybe he wouldn't.

Her right leg rose up, moving slowly, slowly, as she instinctively brought her sex closer to his. She took her mouth from his just long enough to say, "Maybe I don't really need to be wooed."

Hallelujah.

He slipped a hand under her shirt, brushed it against her soft skin up to cup her breast. A silky bra was in the way. His hand slipped to her back, where he deftly unsnapped the annoying under thing.

Before he could move it aside, a voice rang out from the front porch.

"Woo-hoo, Miss Librarian." The front door opened and closed, and quick footsteps headed their way.

Marnie's leg dropped, and she took a step back. So close, and yet...

"There you are!" Janie Holbrook walked into the kitchen with a wide smile on her face and a plastic grocery bag in her hand. Did she realize what she'd interrupted? Perhaps. Perhaps not. "Do you like tomatoes?" she asked, her attention on Marnie. "Of course you do. Everyone likes tomatoes. My garden is bursting with them this year, so I decided to share. Do you have bread? Mayonnaise? There's nothing like a tomato sandwich in the summertime, when the tomatoes are fresh from the garden."

Janie looked at Clint then, and the gleam in her eye hardened. "Maxwell."

Janie was well into her seventies, thin as a rail, and qualified as the nosy neighbor every town seemed to have. She had a massive garden, and a greenhouse almost as big as Marnie's bedroom.

He really didn't need to think about Marnie's bedroom…

She had also been best friends with Jenna's grandmother. Hence the glare.

Janie introduced herself to Marnie and pointed out her house, which was directly across the street. She literally pointed, though they could not see the house from here in the kitchen. Hers was the only one of those three houses currently occupied. Marnie squirmed a little. It should be no surprise that she squirmed. Her bra was hanging loose, thanks to him.

She thanked Janie for the tomatoes, and said with appropriate enthusiasm that she loved tomato sandwiches. Clint had a fleeting hope that Janie would say goodbye after that, but she didn't. She walked to the back porch to look out over Marnie's back yard and make suggestions as to what should be planted there in the fall, and how the roses should be tended.

Would Marnie be here in the fall?

Marnie sighed and followed Janie to the porch, but before she reached the old woman Clint grabbed her arm. He leaned down, placing his mouth near her ear. "Dinner. My house. Saturday night. Prepare to be wooed."

Prepare to be wooed. Those words echoed through Marnie's mind as she walked to work on Friday morning. She wore sneakers for the short trip, but had a pair of navy pumps in her oversized bag, along with her laptop, her smaller purse, and a tomato sandwich, which she intended to have for lunch. She only yawned three or four times.

Last night's monkey brain — and memory turds — had not included Bigfoot. Well, not much. Instead she had laid in bed far too late thinking about Clint and that kiss. She'd been ready to take him there on the kitchen table, until the tomato-toting neighbor had interrupted.

Just as well that they had been interrupted, she thought as she approached the library door. She didn't need to be making rash decisions, especially not where men were concerned. Clint was not at all what she had planned for the man in her life. Mr. Darcy he was not. Sophisticated? No. He had significantly more brain power than Jay or any of her other previous boyfriends had possessed, but he used it to write stories that scared her witless.

That was it. He and the intruder had scared her witless. That's why she couldn't think straight, at least where he was concerned.

Boyfriend. Huh. She could not see Clint as anyone's boyfriend. Lover, yes. Significant other, maybe. Other half…

And on Saturday night, he was going to woo her. He would probably feed her tomato sandwiches and woo her right out of her pants. She should cancel the date here and now. Her dignity was at stake, after all.

Who was she kidding? After yesterday she had no dignity left. She just had an itch that made her wonder why Clint was waiting until Saturday to woo her. She wouldn't mind being wooed right now.

Unlocking the library door after yesterday's excitement gave her a moment's pause. The note had been terrifying! There had been nothing else but that note, so maybe it had been a prank, as Clint had suggested. A sick prank, but still, she was not in danger.

She was not in danger.

She was not in danger.

It became a mantra as she prepared for the day.

Marnie didn't think today would be any busier than the first few days had been, but tonight was the reception to welcome her to town, so she expected Susan to be around in the afternoon, making preparations for the event. Was it an event? Probably not. There was unlikely to be more than a handful of locals, punch, and finger sandwiches. Pimento cheese. Maybe chicken salad.

And Clint. Susan had specifically mentioned their local author when she'd proposed the welcoming event.

Getting involved with Clint, or anyone else, was a bad idea. It had just been a few weeks since she'd ended her relationship with Jay. Ending it had been her idea, but still, she should take time to contemplate her next romantic step. Then again, wasn't every girl allowed a rebound guy and some mind-blowing sex before moving forward in a more thoughtful and sedate manner?

She hadn't had time to check her email at home this morning, since after a restless night she'd overslept. Once she was settled at the front desk, the door unlocked and ready for the patrons she didn't expect to materialize, she opened her laptop, connected to the library Wi-Fi, and clicked the appropriate keys. She planned to stay right here where she could see the front door, while she was on the computer. Eventually she'd have to go to the restroom, taking her well away from the library entrance, but there was nothing to be done for that. She could lock the door for those short trips, she imagined. Just to be on the safe side.

There was a long email from her friend Chelsea, bemoaning again the fact that Marnie had left Birmingham, and going on about the latest in a string of unacceptable boyfriends. Chelsea had worse luck with men than Marnie did.

There was also a message from her mother, which had no information to offer. Just questions, in response to Marnie's email about the move. *Have you made friends? What's the house like? Are you eating?* As if that had ever been a problem!

What her mother didn't ask was *Are you about to sleep with a man you just met?*

Marnie scanned the subject headers, searching amongst the

ads and spam for a response from the Bigfoot expert, Lovell. Nada. Just as well. The more she thought about it, the more she became convinced her imagination had run amok. On the way into town it had been hot, and the flat tire had flustered her. She should not be shocked that the stress of the move combined with that unpleasant excitement had caused her to hallucinate the creature a second time, beyond her back fence. Could've been a shadow that set off her imagination, maybe even a bear. There were more and more bear sightings in the news lately.

Her logical brain told her there was no such thing as Bigfoot. She was *usually* logical.

As she closed her laptop and stored it on a low shelf, she dismissed all logic and started thinking about what she might wear tomorrow night...

CHAPTER 10

Clint had planned to go to the library well ahead of the welcome reception, but he didn't. The shift was close; it was all but upon him. His spine tingled. His limbs itched and his heart raced. He didn't lose control anymore, he shifted only when he wanted to, but somehow Marnie had stirred him up, deep down. He'd allowed a woman he barely knew to turn his life upside down.

When he was stressed, he turned to the forest. Nothing soothed him the way a long run in his Dyn Gwallt form did.

Still, he hadn't lost control in a very long time, and he wouldn't now.

He accepted and even liked who he was, what he was, but he'd worked to gain complete control. When that tingle at his neck came, he was able to stop it. He had learned to tell the creature inside himself, "Later. Be patient. Your time will come but not here, not now." It was uncomfortable but here, in the place that was and always would be his home, he was who and what he wanted to be.

He did that now; he reasoned with the creature. He tamped down the instinct to shift. The pain, the urge, they would go away soon enough. After a few uncomfortable moments he gave up. Why deny himself? The lava tingled down his spine. He cursed out loud, but the sound was garbled.

Giving in to what was coming, Clint stripped down and threw his clothes onto his bed. He opened the french doors and stepped onto the deck, which had a view of the woods. The deck he'd built himself was a great place for coffee in the morning, for reading, for working, and for embracing who he was.

When the hair started to grow, it tickled. Then, for a few seconds, it actually hurt. His legs grew longer, and that hurt a little, too. He was accustomed to the pain, and did not mind it. When his penis drew entirely into his body it didn't hurt, but the sensation was odd, like no other he had ever experienced. He was tall as a man, but the creature was taller by close to two feet. His hands grew bigger, his face longer.

When the shift was complete, Clint whooped once and then leapt over the deck railing. He landed gently, for one of his size, and ran deeper into the woods.

This was what he loved most about who he was. He was strong, he was fast, he was a part of nature as much as the trees around him and the river he ran toward. In spite of his weight he made little noise, and still birds and other small beings fled, they scattered to escape the unnatural creature who had invaded their home.

No, *his* home. Clint Maxwell might be a successful author, he might sometimes try to deny who he was, but when he ran through the woods in this state he felt as if he belonged. He was free. He was king of this forest. He was Dyn Gwallt. And no matter how he wished it to be so, Marnie would never accept this part of him.

He dismissed all thoughts of the librarian and ran.

Marnie wasn't sure what she'd expected from the welcome reception, but this definitely wasn't it.

There were four town council members in attendance, in addition to Susan Tisdale. Two of them were the rude old coots she'd seen in Harry's bar Monday night, and they were no friendlier on Friday than they'd been on Monday. Susan introduced them simply as Jim and George. Marnie wasn't sure she'd be able to tell them apart, in a pinch. Both were gray-haired and of a similar age. They were wiry but not much taller than she was, and they had deeply wrinkled faces and what seemed to be permanent scowls. And the way they stared! She went to the restroom once to check and see if she had food stuck in her teeth, maybe a bit of tomato from her lunch. She did not.

She'd thought the refreshments might consist of punch, nuts, and mints, maybe finger sandwiches, but no. Even though Susan looked and acted normal enough, she definitely did not throw a normal party.

That's what it was, really; a party. There was wine, and a big pitcher of cucumber water for those who didn't like wine. Who didn't like wine? Marnie really, really wanted wine, but she started off with a big glass of the water. She didn't want to be known as the tipsy librarian. There was also a big tub of ice filled with beer situated near the front desk. Jim and George had walked directly to that tub after they'd been introduced. Marnie could almost bet that tub of beer was the only reason they'd come. They certainly hadn't been interested in meeting her.

The food consisted of a platter of huge sandwiches, two cheese pizzas, onion rings, and — as the stash grew — enough wine to supply half of Birmingham with a decent buzz. People came into the library, finally. Some introduced themselves and said hello, while others ignored her. She suspected they were here for the alcohol. The critter guy arrived, said hello and shook her hand, ate and then disappeared. Gabi was there with baby

Mia. Like Marnie, she went with the cucumber water but obviously wanted the wine.

They talked for a few minutes, but when the baby got fussy Gabi excused herself. Marnie walked to the door with her, sad to see a woman she might be friends with go so soon, and discovered that the party had seeped out onto the sidewalk and even into the street. She hadn't seen anywhere near this many people during her days in Mystic Springs. Free alcohol and food were apparently what it took to get the residents to the library. She glanced up and down the street. Well, at least close to the library.

More pizza and sandwiches appeared; the wine and beer were both refreshed. Someone set up a small but impressive sound system in front of the hardware store and cranked up the music, and dancing began. In the street. Where had all these people come from?

Marnie had not met the mayor of Mystic Springs, or even heard her name mentioned, but the older lady was present tonight. Frannie Smith wore a tiara atop frizzy, obviously dyed, black hair. She'd chosen to wear a red silk dress for the occasion. The tiara sat crookedly on her head, and the dress was a size or two too large. The hem dragged on the ground, perhaps because she wore no shoes. She carried a small cake in wrinkled hands.

The reception had been intended to welcome Marnie, or at least that's what she'd been told, but this looked like a street fair. Did these take place often, she wondered? Would any old excuse for a party do?

Marnie looked for Clint, but didn't see him anywhere. That was disappointing, more disappointing than it should be considering that she'd just met him. She didn't know him well enough to be crushed that he wasn't here, even though they'd kissed and she'd considered sleeping with him soon. Very, very soon. Tomorrow, after she'd been properly wooed.

His disturbing absence finally drove her to the wine. Merlot was her favorite, and thank the heavens there were a couple of big bottles just waiting for her. She poured a big glass. She would've thought plastic cups would be used at a party like this one, but no. A folding table had been set with rows of nice, long-stemmed crystal. That table was on the sidewalk right outside the library door. It seemed like a dangerous setup, but so far nothing had been broken.

She took a long drink, determined to be careful not to drop the fine crystal. When that glass was empty, she poured another. Why worry about getting tipsy in a crowd where at least eighty percent were already there, or beyond?

She turned around to look in the other direction for the missing Clint, and found herself face to face with the Mayor. Marnie jumped a little, and some Merlot splashed on her blouse and onto the sidewalk. That was *not* the impression she wanted to make.

Frannie Smith smiled widely and lifted the cake so that it almost touched Marnie's nose. "I made this just for you," the mayor said with a lilt of joy in her wavering voice.

The cake looked and smelled delicious. That was cream cheese icing, if she wasn't mistaken. Dammit, she'd been thinking of cake since she got into town and finally, here it was. Still, it would take two hands to hold the cake properly, and Marnie didn't want to loosen her hold on the wine glass. She was considering her options, and thinking of having cake for breakfast in the morning, when Clint swooped in and took the tempting offering from the mayor's hands.

"That looks fantastic," he said, and then he dropped the cake onto the sidewalk. Icing side down. "Darn. I'm so clumsy."

Mayor Frannie sighed, looked up at Clint, and then shook her finger. "You always were a troublemaker."

"No argument there." He smiled, and then he took Marnie's arm and led her away from the mayor, back toward the library. When they were several feet away, he whispered, "If she brings you another cake, take it, thank her, and then throw it away."

Marnie laughed. "That bad?"

"Worse than you can imagine. Promise me you won't eat it." He opened the door for her and stepped back to allow her to enter ahead of him.

Confused, she promised.

They had the library to themselves. The food and drink — all but the cucumber water — and the people, had all moved outside as the sun set and the day cooled. Still, the air conditioning felt good.

"About tomorrow night…" Clint began. He plucked the wine glass from her hand and placed it on the front desk, where she sat day after day waiting for the residents of this weird town to come in and pick out a freakin' book.

Marnie spun around, her heart pounding, her body tingling from head to toe. "I know what you're going to say." She went up on her toes and kissed him lightly before adding. "I don't want to wait, either."

CHAPTER 11

HE'D WALKED to the library with every intention of calling off their scheduled date, and here he was with Marnie wrapped around him. She'd all but dragged him to the history aisle, where they'd be out of sight if anyone came through the front door. No one was likely to intrude. The fun was all beyond this room. Well, not *all*...

Muted noises from the party on the street seemed far away, as Marnie touched him, kissed him, lifted one leg to wrap around his.

There was not a single coherent word left in Clint's head, and it wasn't because the shift was coming, not this time. It was her. She robbed him of his senses, made him want to take chances he should not, could not, take.

One of her hands settled over his zipper, and a thought stopped him cold. "I don't have a condom with me."

"I'm on the pill."

He wondered why but didn't ask, and still she continued.

"I had a serious boyfriend for a while, and just kept on with the precaution." She looked up at him, those big brown eyes so deep and filled with wanting that he almost melted to the floor. "You didn't think I was a virgin, did you?"

"No."

That hand over his zipper stroked. "I don't want to wait, not even until tomorrow night. I want you, Clint. Here and now."

Maybe he'd come here with doubts about Marnie and what she was doing to him, maybe he had come into town with the best of intentions, but he was no saint, and dammit he wanted her, too. "We could go…"

She unfastened his jeans. "Here and now. I'm pretty sure it won't take long."

Her hand slipped inside his unzipped jeans and he dismissed everything but Marnie and what they both wanted. No, this wouldn't take long at all.

He would not lay her on the floor. She deserved better. She deserved a soft bed and hours of attention. But they didn't have a bed, and they didn't have hours. He reached beneath her skirt and slipped her underwear down and off. She shimmied his jeans down. When he lifted her off her feet, she laughed, and then she moaned.

Her legs around his waist, her arms around his neck, they came together. There was no more laughter, just an intense relief to finally be joined, and then a gentle motion, a sigh, and a drive to the end.

She was his, he felt it to the bottom of his soul. All his doubts melted away. Marnie was wrapped around him, lost in desire as he was. There was nothing but this. It was meant to be. She was his, now and forever. He didn't just fuck Marnie, he claimed her as his own. With every thrust, he claimed her.

She came fast and hard, throwing her head back and crying out softly. Only then did he allow himself to do the same.

He held her in his arms for a long moment. Their hearts pounded; they'd both worked up a sweat. The desire that had driven them had faded, but it was not gone. He suspected it might never be gone.

"I've never had sex in the library before," she whispered.

"Neither have I."

She moved her head back so she could look him in the face. He did not put her down. Not yet. "I imagine it will all be downhill from here," she teased, as she gently brushed the hair off his forehead.

He was not in the mood for teasing. A low growl escaped right before he assured her, "Don't bet on it."

Marnie cleaned herself in the restroom, checked her hair — which was a mess — and her lipstick — which was also a mess. She made repairs as best she could. What had come over her? She'd never been so impulsive. It was out of character for her to jump a man's bones with such abandon. She could blame the wine, she supposed. The wine and the weirdness of this place, the party and the music. And Clint. He drove her nuts in a way no other man ever had. Just the sight of him made her a little crazy.

Crazy enough to stay in Mystic Springs?

He waited for her outside the restroom door. She was a mess, but he looked none the worse for wear. Of course, his hair was shorter than hers and he didn't wear makeup, so there was that. He just stood there, casual as you please, his arms crossed over his chest, his eyes pinned on her. And there it was again, that deep and undeniable response.

She wanted him again. And again.

A young man Marnie had not yet met ran toward them, and for a moment she wondered if something was wrong. He definitely looked distressed. But the guy ran into the men's room, shouting an explanation as he went. "Too much beer!"

It had not even occurred to her that someone might walk in on them while they'd been occupied. Anyone going to the restrooms in the back of the library might've walked past the ancient history section and gotten an eyeful. It was testament to the depth of her desire for Clint that she had not even thought of that. Then again, maybe it was the wine... yes, always blame the wine...

"I'm taking you home," Clint said, his voice low and determined.

Marnie's heart skipped a beat. "Mine or yours?"

"Yours is closer."

She should've cleaned her bedroom this morning...

"When the Milhouse kid is out of the restroom, you're going to see him out and lock the front door, and I'll walk you home."

"The party..."

"Is winding down."

"It's for me so I really should..."

"The residents of Mystic Springs will jump on any excuse for a block party. I promise, their feelings won't be hurt if you leave the festivities a little early. Most of them won't even notice."

No, they hadn't come here for her, she realized that. "I should help clean up. There's such a mess out there."

Clint looked at her hard for a moment. "You should let me take you home where I will pay you the attention you deserve for the next few hours."

Marnie's heart skipped a beat, again. Her insides fluttered and between her legs... that was a bit more than a flutter. There were reasons she should stay away from Clint, but at the moment she couldn't think of even one. "Okay." The Milhouse boy exited the restroom. Marnie took the red-headed kid's arm and walked with him to the front door. If she all but dragged him along, well, it wasn't her fault that the boy was slow.

Long after midnight, Clint was still awake. Marnie slept beside him. She was a cuddler. He'd never been much of a cuddler himself, but where this woman was concerned, he liked it.

Her bedroom was a bit cluttered for his taste, but he liked it because it was all Marnie. The scent, the colors, the shoes and the clothes… it was all *her*. Her bed, her most private space, the air she breathed. He reached out and stroked her hip, and in response she scooted closer to him. She didn't wake up, she simply sighed and shuddered before her breathing returned to a deep, easy rhythm of sleep.

He wouldn't wake her, much as he'd like to, but if she came awake on her own he wouldn't let her go back to sleep too soon. No, he'd kiss her, stroke her, and then he'd be inside her again. He willed her to wake up but she didn't, so he watched her sleep.

If this continued, and there was no reason to think it wouldn't, eventually he would have to tell her the truth. How would she take it? She might be relieved to know she hadn't been hallucinating when she'd seen him. She might be horrified and head straight out of town. If this was more than a fling, and he thought it might be, she would have to know what he was.

It had been a long time since he'd thought of a woman this way, since he'd pondered what an actual relationship might look like.

Even if he could hide the truth from her, a permanent relationship would eventually mean children, most likely, and he could not surprise her with a child who would go hairy in his teenage years. He also remembered his mother talking about some of her strange symptoms during pregnancy. If this turned into more, Marnie would have to go into it with full knowledge of what she was getting into.

But not today.

Marnie sighed in contentment. This was a nice way to come awake in the pre-dawn hours, with Clint's lips on her neck and his strong arms around her. His skin was hot; so was hers. You'd think they'd be tired of one another by now; they were not.

He rolled her onto her back and then he was inside her. She needed him, wanted him. She would never get enough of him. For a moment she looked up at his face. She could barely see him, since the sun was not yet up, but light from a nightlight in the hall, and from the bathroom — had she left it on last time when she'd gotten up a couple of hours ago? — allowed her to study him.

Had she once thought he was not beautiful? He was. Hard, rough, big, and beautiful. And the way he made love to her... she was no virgin, and no one would expect her to be at her age and with a couple of serious relationships under her belt, but she had never experienced anything like this. There had been no awkwardness between them, no hesitation, and to be honest no orgasm had ever hit her so hard. Four times.

Five.

Marnie made a very un-sexy noise, in the heat of the moment. Clint growled, as he was prone to do. The sex was so good, so overwhelming and somehow *alarming*, a surprising *I love you* came to her lips. Fortunately, she was quick enough to stop it from escaping, even though her brain was muddled and still entirely — *almost* entirely — on how his skin felt against hers, how he fit with her as if they'd been made for each other, how warm and wonderful this moment was.

She liked Clint and she loved the way he made her feel, but it was far too soon to even think that she might be in love with him. Love at first sight had never worked out well for her. It was fiction, and belonged in the romance section of the library. And still, she wondered...

"You're kind of amazing," she whispered.

He smiled down at her. "So are you."

I love you.

I love you, too.

No, not yet. They had time. They had all the time in the world for *I love you.*

CHAPTER 12

AFTER A QUICK BREAKFAST and half a pot of coffee, Marnie and Clint rushed out of the house. She'd showered and put on a fresh clean outfit and some makeup. Clint had joined her in the shower, but wore yesterday's clothes since he didn't have any at her house. Would he? Soon? She would be glad to make room for his clothes in her closet. She'd even give him a drawer, if it meant he'd sleep over on a regular basis. It was possible a neighbor might see them leaving together, but she didn't care. She was a grown woman, unattached and available for forming what might be a serious relationship with the local hunk.

Clint insisted on walking her to the library. He didn't really need to insist, because no way would she argue the point. She liked his company. It was nice to have him beside her, wonderful to understand that he wanted to be there on this beautiful morning.

Saturday was a half day at the library. What would she and Clint do this afternoon? Well, besides…

She'd never been so decadent, so *impulsive*. She liked it.

Decadent or not, she was determined that there would be no sex in the library. Not again. It was undignified, and very much unlike her. The sex had been great, but if she hadn't drunk so much wine she never would've given in to the attraction that had overwhelmed her when she'd seen Clint.

Another reason to be thankful for wine.

After a week with only a handful of Mystic Springs residents visiting the library, she was surprised to see a man waiting at the door. He paced, but casually, indolently. He didn't appear to be impatient, just a bit ADHD. She had not seen him before, not even last night at the block party/reception.

For a moment she wondered if he was part of a cleaning crew. Not a single cup or crumb remained on the street or sidewalk. There was no evidence that a party had taken place here last night. But no, he didn't look at all like a janitor or trash collector.

The man was tall, but not as tall as Clint — who was? — and had longish, curling dark hair that was mostly caught up in a man bun. Not her favorite hairstyle on a man, but some could pull it off. His build was slender but not thin, and his clothes were definitely odd. Almost every man around here wore blue jeans. This man's trousers were black, and not made of denim. He wore black boots and a jacket that had to be too warm in this heat. He turned to face her, his movements languid as if he didn't have a care in the world. And was that... a brocade vest? A *waistcoat*?

The man smiled as she approached. Holy cow, he was pretty. Not handsome, not manly in the traditional sense, but pretty.

"Who's that?" Clint asked in a lowered voice.

"You don't know?" Marnie responded. "I figured he was a..." What had Clint called the locals? Ah, yes. "A Springer."

"Nope."

"There you are," the man said. "You must be Marnie Somerset. At least I hope you are."

He had a British accent. *That* was unexpected. If she were a shallow person...

"I am."

113

The man offered his hand, and she took it. Up close, she finally recognized him from his picture.

"I'm Nelson Lovell. I came as soon as I could. Pleased to meet you."

Clint didn't let it show that he recognized the name, but he did. Nelson Lovell, Bigfoot hunter.

Marnie looked a little surprised by Lovell's presence at her place of work, but not much. She wasn't shocked, and she knew exactly who and what he was. "I thought you might respond by email. I really didn't expect you to come here."

"I was in Atlanta speaking at a conference, so it was no trouble to pop over." Lovell smiled at her, and then he looked to Clint.

"This is my friend, Clint Maxwell," Marnie said. "I haven't even told him what I saw." She looked back and up at him, and she blushed. She hadn't blushed when he'd fucked her in the library, or when she'd climbed on top of him in her bed.

But she blushed now.

Marnie had called in a Bigfoot hunter. She'd screwed him senseless and made him believe she belonged to him in a primal and undeniable way. She'd smiled and touched and teased and laughed, and then she'd brought his greatest fear to his damn door. He'd been so sure she was the one, that she was special, that she was different, but this proved he'd been wrong.

Nelson fucking Lovell.

He wasn't even a very good writer.

Marnie unlocked the library door and invited them both in with the promise of coffee. Clint's initial instinct was to decline and run for home, but he didn't. Marnie walked in, Lovell right behind her, and Clint brought up the rear.

The air conditioning felt nice. Clint focused on the cool air as he worked to calm himself down. He needed calm now, he needed the control that normally came to him so easily.

There were a few signs of last night's party inside the library, but since the festivities had moved outside pretty early, it wasn't much. A few cups. One almost empty bottle of wine. A half-empty jug of water with soggy cucumbers floating in it. That might be the remains of a stale sandwich on the end of the front desk. Whoever had taken care of the cleanup outside would've been careful to leave the library as it had been when Marnie had left, locking the door behind her.

Lovell turned his attention to Clint as Marnie headed upstairs at a brisk pace.

"I was excited to receive Miss Somerset's email about her sightings. It's been a couple of years, but hers is not the first Bigfoot sighting from this area."

Clint's response was a grunt.

"How dreadful it must have been for her to see such a creature."

"Yes, I'm sure it was horrifying," Clint agreed.

"I have several days before my next engagement," Lovell said. "And honestly, I have nothing on my schedule that can't be postponed. I'd like Miss Somerset to show me precisely where she saw the creature. I didn't notice a hotel as I drove into town. Do you know of a bed and breakfast or a room to rent for a few days? A week, perhaps."

A lot could happen in a week. He'd known Marnie less than a week, and look where they were.

Where were they, exactly? He'd thought he knew, but now...

"I can't think of any place, other than Eufaula."

"I drove through that town on my way here. It looked charming."

He managed to make the word "charming" sound like an insult. A few minutes of uncomfortable silence followed. Nelson fucking Lovell. Clint tried not to growl, he really did.

Marnie walked down the stairs, a tray bearing three cups of coffee, sugar, and creamer in her hands. She walked carefully, since her hands were full and her heels were high. "Oh, I'm sure there's someone in town who would put Mr. Lovell up for a few days."

The upstairs room wasn't that far away, and the door had been open. She'd probably heard their entire conversation.

"I'll call Susan and ask her for a recommendation," she added.

Lovell put too much sugar in his coffee, but ignored the creamer. Marnie fixed her own coffee. She'd need it. She hadn't gotten much sleep last night.

Clint ignored his cup and asked, "Why don't you tell me what this is about, Marnie?"

He knew, he knew damn well what this was about, but he wanted to hear it in her words.

She took a sip of coffee. "I didn't tell you, or anyone else, because I didn't want you to think I was crazy. On my way into town, I saw a monster. It was hairy and grotesque, and all I could think of was Bigfoot. It looked like every drawing or grainy photo I've even seen. I tried to dismiss what I'd seen as a hallucination, or my imagination, but then I saw it again, in the woods behind my house."

Monster. Grotesque.

"I did some research and came upon Mr. Lovell's book on the subject. When I emailed him I hoped he might respond, but I didn't think he'd actually show up."

The Bigfoot hunter smiled. "Miss Somerset, you must call me Nelson. I'm sure we'll become great friends."

She smiled back. "And I'm Marnie. Trust me, these days I can use all the friends I can get!" She laughed, and glanced back at Clint with a twinkle in her eye.

Clint backed away, one step, as if her gaze had the power to burn him. "I need to get home."

"Stay," Marnie said softly.

He shook his head.

"I'll be closing up at noon. Maybe we can..."

"You'll be busy getting Mr. Lovell settled and showing him where you saw your grotesque monster." He took another step back, but didn't turn around.

"Tonight..." She began.

"I just remembered, I have other plans for tonight. Sorry."

Her face fell, but then she didn't realize what she'd done. How could she?

A woman he'd allowed himself to consider *his* had brought his greatest nightmare to his home. He could forgive her for calling him a monster, for describing him as grotesque. That was probably true.

But he could not forgive her for bringing Lovell to Mystic Springs. Sadly for her, he would not be the only one who wouldn't forgive.

Nelson Lovell looked exactly like the picture on the back of his book. If anything, he was more handsome, and he was definitely younger looking. He probably wasn't much older than she was. He had thick dark hair any woman would kill for, a perfectly symmetrical face, and dark eyes that studied her intently when she spoke. It was obvious he paid great attention to her every word.

And the accent! It was mesmerizing. Very Mr. Darcy-like.

Wasn't he from Oregon? That was what his bio said. Maybe he'd moved there and brought his sexy British accent with him.

There weren't many library patrons on this fine summer morning, but Marnie was pleased to see even a handful. Maybe Saturday morning was prime time for the Mystic Springs Library. During a lull in the activity, she called the only person she could think of, the only local number she had in her cell phone.

Susan Tisdale did not seem thrilled with Marnie's question, but she did pass along a phone number for a bed and breakfast. Marnie was pleased but surprised to find out that there were rooms to rent anywhere in Mystic Springs. It wasn't exactly a tourist destination, and considering how welcomed she'd been among the Springers, she could only imagine how a visitor might be treated.

She would be helpful and friendly to Nelson, even if others were not.

The Riverside Rest B&B owner, Elaine Forrester, was happy to hear from Marnie and said she'd prepare a room for her new guest right away.

Marnie straightened the little bit of mess that remained from last night's reception, tossing away leftovers and wiping down her desk, as well as a table that had been used for cucumber water and sandwiches. She toted what was left of the cucumber water back to the bathrooms to dump down the drain. The container was heavy, but she managed.

Nelson didn't offer to help; he walked the aisles perusing books while she worked, but that was alright. It wasn't his job to clean up her mess, she reasoned.

Clint would've offered, she suspected.

Now and then Nelson asked about what she'd seen, but they were always interrupted and she never got far. Felicity returned her books and picked up two more. Marnie didn't think it was her imagination that the little girl with the sunny disposition glared at Nelson Lovell.

Gabi, baby on her hip, stopped in to return a book she'd picked up a couple of days ago. She was on the run, about to head to her shop. The look she gave Lovell wasn't a glare at all. It was the look of a single woman admiring a handsome man. She didn't speak to him, though, she just admired the view for a moment.

After phone calls had been made and the mess from the reception was cleared, a couple of other people stopped in. No one stayed very long, but they did seem to arrive just as she and Nelson were getting into serious conversation.

By the time all that was done, it was almost time to close the library for the day. Lunchtime. Marnie locked the front door a mere two minutes early, and walked with Nelson across the street to Eve's. She looked up and down the street, wondering if she'd see Clint, wondering why his attitude had changed so abruptly. She'd been looking forward to their date tonight, but maybe after last night he didn't see any reason to cook dinner for her.

He probably didn't see any reason to woo a woman who'd so enthusiastically jump his bones in her place of work. Too bad. She'd bet he was a great wooer.

There would be time to figure out what had happened with Clint, and fix it if she could, once she'd seen to Nelson. She couldn't imagine that he'd be here more than a couple of days.

As always, the aroma that hit Marnie as she walked into Eve's was welcoming and tantalizing and made her stomach rumble. "Everything here is so good. You just wait."

She sat on one side of a booth and Nelson took the other. As usual, Eve was there right away to take their order. *Not* as usual, she pursed her lips and frowned.

"I'll have the special, whatever it is," Marnie said. "And sweet tea."

"Chicken pot pie," Eve said without further elaboration. Then she turned to Nelson, who said,

"Do you have a vegan menu?"

Eve blinked twice. "No."

"Vegan is…" Nelson began.

"I know what vegan means," Eve interrupted sharply. "Just don't have a special menu. How about a salad?"

"Lovely. I'll have that with oil and vinegar on the side, and a glass of water. No ice."

Eve huffed. "Sounds delish." Before Nelson could respond, she walked away.

Nelson looked around the cafe, which was not particularly busy even though it was noon. The Bigfoot hunter grimaced a little, as if he found the place unpleasant. Maybe Eve's Cafe was plain, it was certainly not fancy, but if he'd actually try the food, he'd change his tune.

"The food here is great," Marnie said. "It's normally pretty busy at lunchtime." She suspected many of the usual customers were at home, sleeping off the effects of last night's party.

Nelson made a low sound that was kind of a scoff, then he said, "Our waitress is rather a bitch, don't you think?"

Marnie was surprised by his words, which were delivered in that lovely accent but with a bite she didn't care for. She didn't say so. "Eve's not usually so rude. She must be having a bad day."

He smiled. It *was* a very nice smile. "Everyone is allowed, I suppose." His tone shifted, became friendlier, not so snobbish. He leaned over the table a bit, and the smile widened. "Now, tell me all about your sightings. After we eat, we'll check out the locations. I want to get a few pictures before the camera crew arrives."

Eve slapped a tall glass of tea and another of water — no ice — on the table. When she was gone again, Marnie whispered, "Camera crew?"

"Didn't I mention it?" Nelson brushed a strand of hair away from his face with long, elegant fingers. "I'm filming a new show for a well-known cable network. I'm not yet at liberty to share the details, but trust me, you will be impressed. The first episode won't air for six months, which is why you haven't heard of it. I'm quite excited. There aren't many shows out there with cryptozoologists at the helm, and the others are, well, rather substandard."

"I didn't realize…"

He grinned at her. "Smile, Marnie. You're about to be a star."

"I don't want to be a star." She'd just wanted someone to tell her that she wasn't crazy.

"You'll be brilliant," he said. "Will your large and rather quiet friend be joining us on our excursion?"

"Clint? No, I don't think so."

"Is he…" Nelson waved one hand to the side, "Your boyfriend? A significant other? Just a friend?"

Marnie sighed. That was a question she was still asking herself. "To be totally honest, I'm not sure."

"You're a beautiful and intelligent woman. I'm sure you can do better."

What the hell did that mean? Clint was a good man, a good (if slightly twisted) writer, and though she would not tell Nelson, he was also the sexiest man she'd ever known. He was lumberjacky at first glance, that was true, but what was wrong with that? Nothing. Nothing at all.

Before she could come up with a response, Eve placed a large bowl of lettuce in front of Nelson. There were two cherry tomatoes, as well as a few soggy looking slices of cucumber, on top. Those slimy things might've come straight out of the much-maligned cucumber water. The oil and vinegar were set to the side, as requested. It looked nothing like the fantastic salad she'd eaten here, a couple of days ago.

Marnie's own chicken pot pie looked much better.

Nelson pursed his lips as he studied her meal with disdain. Then he sighed and said, "You know, the camera adds at least ten pounds."

Her initial response, which remained unspoken, was *bite me*.

CHAPTER 13

CLINT'S PLAN was to go home, shift, and run the woods for hours. He rarely experienced rage, but when he did that was his response. The freedom of embracing who he was at his core soothed his soul.

He'd only felt this way two times in his life. After his parents had died, and when he'd found out Jenna had been trying to change him.

Dammit, a woman he had just met should not have the power to break his heart and his spirit, to drive him to this.

He sometimes wondered if he was more man or beast. What had he been born to be? Which was his true natural state? Since he'd been born human and had remained that way for fifteen years before he'd shifted for the first time, it would seem that was his nature. But at times like these he felt as if Dyn Gwallt was his true self, as if he were truly himself only when he embraced the beast.

Tempted as he was, he didn't immediately head for home. He went into the hardware store and browsed a bit. Luke seemed distracted, and didn't have anything set aside for Clint, so they barely spoke. When that was done, he went into Ivy's bakery and bought two bear claws and a big cup of coffee. She didn't bother him while he sat at one of her tiny tables and consumed it all.

That done, he headed down to the beauty shop to see if Gabi had a moment to trim his hair, but she was booked. This was a sparsely populated town, for sure, but Saturday was the hairdresser's busiest day. He could've waited, but he didn't. He wanted to be on the street, needed to be there.

He left Main Street briefly, walking with purpose toward the Mayor's house. He knocked on the door forcefully. She was slow, but eventually a smiling Frannie Smith, wearing a silky hot pink bathrobe, opened the door and invited him in.

Clint declined to enter the house. "You know why I'm here. No cake for Marnie."

Frannie sighed. "She's going to be trouble, and you know it. Several of us are quite worried."

"I'll take care of it. No more cake. I want your word."

The old woman rolled her eyes and promised she'd lay off the baking, for a while.

Clint hurried back toward Main Street, looking this way and that as he came to the intersection. His eyes lingered on the far south end of the street. It was then that he realized that he was waiting around to see Nelson Lovell leave the library. It wasn't yet noon. The Bigfoot hunter was still there, talking to Marnie. Talking about *him*.

He should go home. He didn't.

After perusing the offerings in the antique store window for a bit, he got an ice cream cone from Jordan's shop. As usual, it was freezing in her place. She seemed to like it that way, no matter the time of year. She smiled as he made his selection, but was quiet, as usual.

Like her father before her, Jordan was the reason that in Mystic Springs, it always snowed on Christmas Eve.

Clint ate his ice cream cone standing on the sidewalk. His truck was close, where he'd parked it last night. He could climb in and head home whenever he felt like it, but he continued to wait. How the hell long was Lovell going to stay in the library?

"Fuck it," he said beneath his breath as he headed for his truck. Time to go home. Past time.

He had the key fob in his hand, but before he could unlock the driver's side door, Susan intercepted him. She appeared out of nowhere, swooping into his path.

She looked unsettled. Nervous. That was not a normal look for her.

"There you are," she said, her voice calm but her eyes... not so much. "I worried when I saw that your truck hadn't moved since yesterday."

He could make up a tale, but why bother? "I spent the night at Marnie's."

"Oh, I see." Susan was savvy, but she wasn't a practiced liar. She knew good and well where he'd been last night.

"But you knew that, didn't you?"

Susan sighed, then glanced down the sidewalk toward a couple that was walking their way, probably heading to the ice cream shop for a treat. "It's impossible to keep a secret in this town. Well, normally." She took his arm and led him across the street to a spot on the sidewalk that was deserted. No one had gathered outside the police station to visit.

Clint couldn't help but remember when downtown had been packed on every summer Saturday. The town really was dying. What would they do when there was nothing left? The idea chilled him.

Still holding on, Susan walked him to the nearest cross street, where she turned. Only then did she drop his arm. He couldn't see the library from here, but what the hell? He wasn't Marnie's keeper, and Lovell was going to be a pain in the ass no matter where he was or how long he hung out at the library.

Was Susan afraid someone would come along and interrupt them if they stayed on Main Street? No one would bother them here, that was certain. The closest house to the left of this quiet street was for sale and had been for a while. Someone from the town council mowed the grass, in order to keep it presentable, and there were a couple of rocking chairs on the wide front porch. That was where Susan took him.

She sat, sighed, and indicated that he should take the chair beside her.

He didn't have time for this, whatever it was. "Look, I…"

She didn't allow him to finish. "Before she was killed, Alice was concocting a potion to do what she's always wanted to do."

Now she had his attention. "Brigadoon?"

"Brigadoon. I didn't think she'd ever manage it, and goodness knows she tried for years, but she finally had it. She found the spell a couple of years ago, but it calls for a formula, a potion of sorts, in order to activate it." Susan looked at him, and it was then that he noticed how tired she was. "If Alice hadn't died, Mystic Springs would have been entirely isolated from the world within a few weeks. Perhaps days."

No one would have ever found Mystic Springs again. No one would have been able to find their way out, either. They'd be trapped, their small town isolated as if it had been completely encased in a snow globe. No way in, no way out. "Is that why she was killed?"

Susan looked out over the recently mowed lawn. "I don't know, but I suppose that's possible."

Again, Clint noted the exhaustion behind Susan's eyes. She was always so calm, or at least she appeared to be. Maybe she just hid her anxiety well.

"She's dead and we're still a part of the world, so what's got you in such a state?"

"Alice is dead, but the formula she concocted to go along with the spell is somewhere in that house. At least, I think it's there. I can almost *feel* it. As you well know there are others, some of the most militant Springers, who would love to get their hands on it and finish what she started."

That was the truth. Alice had not been the only Springer so fed up with the world that they wanted nothing more than to cut themselves — and everyone else — off from it.

Still others wanted to do the opposite, to knock down the bubble that protected Mystic Springs and make them a real and true part of the world. They'd want the formula as well, in order to destroy it so it could never be used.

"I could've placed the new librarian in a number of vacant houses," Susan said, "but I put her in Alice's house so I could go in and out without rousing suspicion."

"So you could search for the spell and the formula. Or do you already have the spell?"

"I found the spell a few months ago, but it was a copy. I'm sure Alice shared it with others. But the formula... I think she kept that to herself. And yes, I've been in and out of the house a number of times, searching for five minutes here, fifteen there. For all the good it's done me. The formula for the potion is there, I know it, I can *sense* it, but I haven't been able to find the damn thing." She looked at him again. "I searched when I was getting the house ready for Marnie, and a couple of times while she was at work. I'd carry in food, or flowers, or something so anyone watching would think my reason for being there was normal council business."

"Susan Tisdale, welcome wagon," Clint grumbled.

She ignored him. "I'm not the only one who knows about Alice's success. I suspect whoever tried to scare Marnie wants her out of the house so they can tear it apart. To find and use the formula or destroy it, I don't know. Could be either one." Susan tried a smile that didn't work. "If you're going to spend time there, you could look around."

"I won't be going back." Harsh words, but true.

Susan looked genuinely surprised. "Why not?"

"She called in a damn Bigfoot hunter. Nelson Lovell."

"Well, shit," Susan drawled. "I should've asked for a name for her 'friend from out of town,' when she called to ask about a place for a visitor to stay. I thought maybe it was a girlfriend from Birmingham, or family in for a visit. She's not close to any of her relatives, I made sure of that before I hired her, but still, family is family." She huffed a bit. "Lovell's presence could complicate things, though he can and will be taken care of."

"The problem isn't what he might find, it's that Marnie called him in."

Susan shrugged. Don't take it personally. "She saw you, she doesn't know it's you, her response is a natural one. You can't blame her for taking action."

Yes, he could. He did. Logical or not, it was a betrayal to bring his greatest fear to his home.

Susan looked him in the eye in an almost censuring way. "I need you to keep seeing her. Find the formula for that potion and destroy it, before someone who wants to use the spell gets their hands on it."

"How many people know about it?"

"A small handful. If word got out, you can only imagine what would happen."

War. The only issue that divided the Springers was that of isolation. Did they continue to be a part of the world, or did they shun everyone who was not like them? A large portion of the residents would welcome a spell that hid them from the rest of the world. Brigadoon, they had always called it. Some said the word with a sneer, others with wistful hope.

"I'll see what I can do."

Susan looked genuinely concerned when she said, "Keep a close eye on Marnie. I'm not sure what lengths those who want what Alice discovered would go to in order to have access to that house. If they find it before we do…"

"You should've thought of that before. Marnie is in danger because you put her in that house. Frannie baked her a cake."

"Well, shit. I'll have a talk with our Mayor."

"I already did."

Susan looked away from him, lost in thought for a long moment. "I did what I thought was best."

He shouldn't care, but the feeling that they could be more, the feeling that Marnie was *the one*, lingered. Betrayal aside, he didn't want to see her hurt.

"You decided that losing a Non-Springer was a risk you were willing to take."

She didn't deny that accusation.

The more Marnie talked to Nelson, the less she liked him. The accent that had initially been so charming became annoying. He complained a lot. About the heat, the food, the people. It wasn't like Mystic Springs was perfect. She'd had her own share of troubles, but she didn't complain about everything and everyone. Did she? If she did, she hoped she didn't sound so petty.

After lunch they walked to her house — she wonderfully full from a fantastic chicken pot pie, Nelson grumbling about the plainness of his salad — where she collected her car keys and her car, which hadn't been driven in almost a week. She drove slowly along Magnolia Road and turned onto Main Street. One more turn ahead, and she'd be heading to the site where she'd first seen Bigfoot.

Along the way Nelson studied the town, commenting often and negatively on its size and lack of activity. Right before she turned off Main Street he pointed out the car he'd driven to town, a ridiculous silver sports car which sat so low to the ground she'd have to crawl in, if she were to ride in it. Which she did not plan to do.

When she reached her destination Marnie parked on the side of the road, on the town side of Harry's — the interior of which she hoped never to see again — and pointed out what she'd seen and where. Nelson stopped complaining and asked a hundred questions. Most of them she had no answer to. He walked into the woods while she stayed on the side of the road, out in the open. She was not going in there, no way. There had been a time when she'd planned to do just that, to walk in the woods, to find her way down to the river not too far from her house. She'd seriously thought about getting a picture of Bigfoot, of seeing the thing up close. What had she been thinking?

Nelson seemed fascinated with the wooded area, though he found nothing of interest.

After that, Marnie drove him back to her house so she could point out the woods where she'd seen the creature the second time. He seemed interested in both settings, but in both he focused on the wooded surroundings rather than the clearings where the beast had been visible.

Nelson walked deep into the woods behind her house, as he had beyond the road where she'd had her flat tire Monday evening, looking for poop. He called it "scat" but that was just a fancy word for poop. He seemed disappointed, so she assumed he didn't find any.

Marnie remained in her back yard, waiting for him to finish his hunt beyond her white picket fence. There had been a time when she'd planned to do just that, to walk in the woods, to find her way down to the river. Her desire to explore had died a slow but certain death.

As she walked the edges of her flower garden, her mind kept returning to Clint. She'd tried for a while not to think about him, but that hadn't worked so why even make the attempt?

She bent down and pulled a pesky weed, then another. Her mind wandered.

Why had he been so annoyed with her? What about Nelson

had set him off? Ok, good looks and sexy accent aside Nelson could be annoying, she'd figured that out already, but Clint had obviously hated the cryptozoologist on sight.

His instincts were better than hers.

At first glance, Nelson Lovell was everything she wanted in a man. Handsome. Cultured. A writer who didn't scare her with vivid descriptions of unnatural beings and nauseating gore. And that accent! But he was also kind of a jerk at times, and honestly, was hunting Bigfoot really a sophisticated career choice?

Watching Nelson walk into the woods with his camera and notebook, she'd realized Bigfoot hunting was not for her. There were more important things in life. Like…

"Where's the asshat?"

Marnie turned toward the familiar voice and smiled. Speaking of more important things. She was so glad to see Clint coming toward her. When he'd walked away this morning she'd honestly wondered if she'd see him again. And here he was, tall and rugged and normal, and carrying a cloth tote bag with celery poking out of the top.

"He's in the woods, looking for poop."

"You didn't want to join him?"

She wrinkled her nose. "It's not really my idea of fun."

He lifted the bag. "Do you like gumbo?"

She smiled. "I do. Who doesn't?" She cocked her head to one side. "I thought you had other plans tonight."

"Changed them," he said simply. "I'm going to put this stuff in your fridge."

"I'll come with you."

"No," Clint said as he turned toward the house. "You stay here, while I get the gumbo started. You wouldn't want to miss a momentous crap discovery."

She watched him walk through her back door, and what could only be relief washed through her. Marnie didn't know how a man, any man, could become so necessary to her in such a short period of time, but Clint had. He was back. Whatever had annoyed him earlier in the day, he'd gotten past it and come back to her.

Everything was going to be ok.

Clint was more important than any supposedly mythical creature. She had meaningful things to take care of, and she was looking at one of them right now.

If Bigfoot would leave her alone, she'd return the favor.

If Alice had hidden her Brigadoon formula in an obvious place, Susan — or someone else — would've found it by now. The vegetables for the gumbo sat on the kitchen counter. It would take a while to prep them all, and he couldn't leave the room while he was making the roux. If he was going to search the house it had to be now, while Marnie was outside and occupied with her Bigfoot hunter.

Clint grumbled as he searched. He was a writer, not a spy. While he, by necessity, had to hide the truth about a part of himself from those outside Mystic Springs, he was otherwise up front and open. He didn't hold back, hated lying or being lied to, so sneaking around someone else's home searching for a hidden formula wasn't exactly his idea of fun. Why had he agreed to take this job, and how far would he go? Would he sleep with Marnie again and search her house while she slept? Could he hide the fact that he was still angry?

No, not angry, not really. He was disappointed. He'd expected more from her. His response was illogical, since he'd only known her for a few days. Yes, they'd had sex, but that didn't mean he knew her as well as he should. Marnie didn't know, couldn't possibly know, that what she'd seen on the road and again in the woods was him, in his other form. Illogical or not, he could not forgive her.

He searched the house not because he was disappointed in Marnie, and not because Susan had asked him to. He did it because he didn't want the town he loved to be removed from the map. The death of the town would still come, if they were completely isolated, it would just be slower and more painful. Springers and Non-Springers alike would have no place to go. The spell would effectively make Mystic Springs a prison.

There was no guarantee that the formula Susan wanted to destroy was even in this house. She said she felt it here, but that was far from an exact science. Alice might've written it down here then hidden a single piece of paper at the library, or buried it in the garden, or secreted it at a friend's house. She could've stashed a note card in one of the vacant storefronts on Main Street.

But it was likely here. Alice would've wanted to keep it close. It was possible she hadn't written it down at all, but had only memorized what she needed to erase Mystic Springs from the map. If that was the case, they would never know. They would always wonder if it was out there, waiting to be found.

Alice was more cautious than that, and since this was something she'd wanted for years, she'd obviously tried before without success. In that case, she'd definitely want the ingredients to her Brigadoon potion saved in writing. Somewhere.

He didn't have time to climb into the attic. That would have to be a search for another day. But he looked quickly and carefully through the bookcase in the parlor. Some of the books there were Marnie's, but others were those Alice had left behind. A single sheet of paper tucked in a book could take a long time to find.

Especially if she'd tucked that paper into one of the books in the Mystic Springs Library.

Just a few minutes in, and he knew this wasn't going to be an easy task. Why him? Why hadn't Susan asked someone with a different kind of magic to have a look around? Because he was the one sleeping with Marnie, that was why. Because he had a reason to be here.

Besides, she didn't want everyone to know what Alice had found and hidden here. If they did Marnie would not be safe. No one would be safe if Springers went to war with one another.

Clint gave up, for the moment, and returned to the kitchen to wash and chop the vegetables. He'd made gumbo many times, it was his favorite food, and he had the prep down to an art. He made quick work of the onions, celery, and bell pepper. Through the kitchen window he saw Marnie and that asshat Lovell walking toward the back porch.

The hairs on the back of Clint's neck stood up. Maybe he wasn't close to a lot of people, but if he had a natural enemy, it was that man and those like him.

As they came in through the kitchen door, Clint slowed his movements considerably. Let them think he'd taken all this time chopping vegetables.

Lovell spoke up, his British accent grating on Clint's nerves. "Marnie tells me you're making gumbo for supper."

Clint turned his head to look at the man and grin. It was likely not a friendly grin at all. "I am. Too bad you can't join us."

"Clint!" Marnie said in a censuring tone of voice.

Lovell help up one hand. "No, no, it's Saturday night and this is a date, I imagine. Though I'm almost positive I heard you cancel your plans for the evening." He glanced around the room, making a bitter face when he saw the sausage sitting on the counter. "Besides, I don't eat meat of any kind, and spicy foods give me terrible indigestion."

"Good to know," Clint growled.

Marnie walked Lovell to the door, while Clint stayed in the kitchen. He'd seen quite enough of the Bigfoot hunter already. Still, he listened closely. Marnie offered Lovell a ride to his car, but he said he would walk. Apparently, he already knew where he was going. Mystic Springs was so small, nothing was particularly difficult to find.

Marnie was back in minutes. She stood in the doorway, still and quiet. He felt her there, *smelled* her. Without looking back, Clint said, "I don't like him."

"That's obvious."

"Lovell grates on my nerves, and I swear, he comes off as so damned phony." He grabbed the shrimp from the fridge, where he'd stashed it before starting his quick and fruitless search. He waited for Marnie to defend the Bigfoot hunter, but that defense never came.

"I can't argue with that," she said.

"He's..."

"I don't want to talk about Nelson Lovell," she interrupted.

Neither did he, but what choice did he have? "What do you want to talk about?"

She moved into the room, came closer, sighed in a slow and easy way that both saddened and soothed him. "I want to talk about why you ran today and cancelled our date. You did show up after all, but for a while there you looked spooked and angry and... I don't know. But you did run, and I don't understand why."

Clint turned, leaning back against the counter so he could look down at her. "This is happening fast."

"It is."

"I'm not a man who's accustomed to fast." Not for a very long time. As an adult he'd learned to be cautious, to be suspicious. He hadn't been suspicious enough where Marnie was concerned.

"I wasn't in your plans," she said. "I get that. Trust me, you weren't in mine, either."

She went up on her toes and kissed him. He would've grabbed her, he *wanted* to grab her, but he didn't. It was nice, a simple kiss.

"I'm going to shower and put on something comfortable," she said as she backed away.

He was relieved to hear she'd be washing the stink of Lovell off her body. His sense of smell was acute whether he was man or beast, and the stench of the Bigfoot hunter lingered. Had Lovell touched her? He didn't think so. The stink was faint, as if they'd done no more than share air. Even that was enough to taint her.

"We can talk when I'm done," Marnie said as she left the kitchen.

Clint didn't say so, but he didn't think they'd be doing a lot of talking tonight.

CHAPTER 14

Marnie couldn't believe she'd ever thought she wanted a Mr. Darcy. What she really wanted, what she'd *always* wanted, was this.

The connection she had with Clint was unexpected. It was raw and powerful. There was nothing sophisticated about him. He was real. Solid. Down-to-earth. A waistcoat wouldn't suit him at all.

What they shared was sex, and the sex was great, but somehow it went beyond the physical. It was love, love that came too fast and unexpected. Somehow what they'd found was also more than love. Clint was quickly becoming as necessary as the air she breathed, as if she'd been incomplete before she'd met him.

She'd never been so aware of the sensation of skin to skin, or of the special scent that was created when they touched. She'd never needed anyone or anything the way she needed him. No kiss had ever rocked her the way his did.

Her brain had definitely been clouded by sex.

Lying in bed, at an early morning hour when she should be sleeping, she cuddled against him. Heavens, he was warm.

Wonderfully warm. She liked it. "I'm glad you changed your plans for the evening."

"So am I."

"I can't imagine anything better than this."

His answering grunt sounded like an agreement.

Marnie rose up a little so she could look Clint in the eye. "You're right, though. This is happening too fast."

The growl that followed was so soft, she felt rather than heard it. "Want me to go?" he asked.

She shook her head. "No. I should, but I don't." She rested her chin on his chest. There was something special about the way her bare body fit against his. "What should we do tomorrow? I have the whole day off."

He caught her eye and held it. "I say we stay right here all day. There's leftover gumbo so we won't starve."

It was a lovely idea. Sex and gumbo. "Sounds like a plan. I just have to see Nelson for a little while, in the afternoon. He wanted me to help him find places for his camera crew to stay while they're here, and..."

"Camera crew?" Clint interrupted.

"Yeah, he's filming a cable show about hunting Bigfoot. Sounds lame to me, but he's very excited."

With a quick flip she was on her back and Clint hovered above her. He was big, hard, and those eyes... she couldn't see them well enough in the dim light, but they were always intense. Alive.

"Get rid of him," he whispered. "Tell him you made it up. Tell him you lied about what you saw."

His intensity should've frightened her, but it didn't. She rested a hand on his side, rubbed her thumb over a muscle there. "But I didn't lie. What's the big deal?"

"Trust me, it's a..." His voice deepened a little, his eyes flashed in what seemed to be anger.

And then he was gone, leaping from the bed in a flash and stalking toward the door. "I'm going for a walk," he mumbled.

Marnie sat up in the bed. "Don't you want your pants?"

He just growled, as he sometimes did, leaving the room and his pants behind, so she assumed... no.

Midnight naked jogging. Yeah, he was definitely *not* Mr. Darcy.

Clint had not intended to run all night, but he was so spun up he'd had no choice. His life was normally so well ordered, so controlled. In the past week it had been anything but. Marnie had gotten too close too fast. Alice's formula could spell disaster for Mystic Springs. Nelson Lovell was bad enough, but a camera crew? A damn TV show about Bigfoot? He could avoid them all, but it would mean being very careful.

He hated being careful.

Nothing and no one made him lose control, but Marnie had pushed him to a breaking point. Could he have tamped down the urge to shift and run? Yes. Did he want to? No.

Would it be easy? Again, no.

As Dyn Gwallt he ran from Marnie's house to the river, then turned and ran along the bank. It was still dark. No Non-Springer boater or fisherman from beyond Mystic Springs would see. If anyone was out there, making their way down the Chatta-hoochee, he would be nothing more than a shadow lost in other, deeper shadows.

As the skies began to turn gray and birds sang, he turned into the forest that was as much his home as any cabin. He wove his way through the thick brush. Normally he took care not to leave a trail of destruction, but at the moment he didn't care about the bushes he trampled, the limbs he broke. As he neared home he climbed an old oak tree, one of his favorites, almost to the top.

There he whooped, not in joy as he normally did, but in frustration.

After a short while he shimmied down the tree, but instead of heading for home or directly back to Marnie's he turned in another direction and ran, attempting to burn off or tamp down the turmoil inside him.

He was free, but he was also trapped. He had allowed a woman to turn his life upside down in a matter of days.

In the pre-dawn hours, Dyn Gwallt stood just beyond Marnie's back fence and looked at the garden, the back porch, the window of her bedroom. This had been Alice's house for a long time, but already it felt more like Marnie's. In short order she'd made it a home, she'd claimed it as her own.

She'd claimed him.

He should go home and hide there, let Susan handle her own problem. He could leave Marnie to the Springers and whatever they decided to do with her.

Could he do that?

The scream took him by surprise. Without thinking, he vaulted over the fence and into Marnie's back yard, and ran for the door.

———

Tired of constantly waking up wondering if Clint had returned and finding his side of the bed empty, Marnie finally gave up on a good night's sleep. Her mind was firmly on the kitchen and a big cup of coffee. Maybe a cookie. She'd pulled on a bathrobe — in case she found Clint sleeping on the couch or sitting in the kitchen — and stepped into the hallway as quietly as possible. Again, in case Clint was sleeping somewhere.

At first she thought what she saw out of the corner of her eye was a weird shadow, but then the shadow — which was shaped like a tall, thin man — turned and looked at her.

The shadowman had removed a painting from the wall in the small dining room between the parlor and the kitchen. The landscape had been hanging there when she'd moved in. It was too dark for her taste, but since she had nothing to hang in its place, it remained. Her eyes were not on the painting, at the moment; it was on the shadow that held the framed painting in one hand and a wicked looking curved knife in the other.

Her initial scream was weaker than she'd like; terror had stolen some of her voice. Like in a dream. A nightmare. She screamed again, louder this time. The shadow calmly set the painting aside. It did not set aside the knife. Heart pounding far too hard, Marnie found her survival instinct and bolted. The shadowman stood between her and the parlor, so she ran toward the back door. Too afraid to look back, she sprinted through the kitchen to the screened-in porch. She pushed through the screen door and vaulted into the back yard.

Where she found herself running straight toward Bigfoot.

It was a nightmare. She was caught between a hairy monster and a menacing shadowman wielding a very real knife. Yes, nightmare, had to be.

No, somehow this was all real.

She couldn't turn back. The shadowman had followed her, she just knew it. Not that she was about to take the time to look back and make sure.

Bigfoot barreled toward her, long strides eating up the distance between them in a hurry. Marnie held her breath. Where could she turn, where could she go? Up close, Bigfoot was even bigger than he'd seemed at a distance. He was also hairier, if that was possible. His eyes met hers; they were surprisingly human. And kind. He had kind eyes. That was unexpected.

All this went through her mind in a split second, before the creature cut to the side and ran past her, toward...

Finally, Marnie stopped and looked back. The shadowman had indeed followed her. He vaulted down the back steps with that curved knife in his hand. That blade had to be eight inches long, and an insubstantial black hand gripped the very real handle as if it knew what to do with that weapon. The thing stopped when it saw Bigfoot. Stopped and took a step back.

The sun was rising. There was light here, plenty of it. She could see the hair on Bigfoot, the flowers in her garden, every detail of her house. She could no longer blame nighttime shadows, stress, or the heat for what she saw.

Bigfoot was very clear, but the shadowman was not. Why couldn't she see that thing's face? Even by the light of day, it remained a dark, indistinct blob.

Instead of running back the way he'd come, the shadow thief ran around the corner of the house. Bigfoot gave chase. In seconds they were both gone.

Marnie considered sitting down right where she stood. Her knees were weak, her heart pounded too hard. Only the prospect of sitting on grass wet with morning dew kept her from plopping to the ground.

She hurried toward the safety of her house, which to be honest didn't feel particularly safe at the moment. As she reached the porch she took the time to lock the screen door. For all the good that would do her. She didn't think that mesh screen would slow Bigfoot or the shadowman man. Still, a locked door made her feel a bit safer.

Marnie made her way into the kitchen on shaky legs. Instead of falling into a kitchen chair or grabbing her cell from the bedroom to call 9-1-1, she went to the coffee maker and started the process of brewing a morning pot. As she waited for it to dispense coffee, her heart slowed. Her knees stopped shaking.

Was it her imagination, or had Bigfoot saved her?

CHAPTER 15

THE DARK FIGURE he'd chased out of Marnie's back yard could not possibly be faster than he was, yet it all too quickly disappeared. By the time he made it to the front yard the dark thing, whatever it was, was gone. Clint, still in his beast form, looked around the area for a few minutes, but even his nose gave him no clue as to where the attacker had gone.

Whatever, whoever it was, the shadow possessed a dark magic that disguised their identity and allowed it to elude him. You'd think in all his years in Mystic Springs he might've seen such a creature, but he had not. The town was lousy with witches, male and female, and he couldn't possibly know the abilities of each and every one.

Not every Springer wanted their friends and neighbors to know what they could do.

Clint explored the yards of the closest houses but found nothing, no clue, no unusual scent.

He returned to Marnie's house, lumbering into her back yard much more slowly than he'd left it. Given the hour he could, and should, run home, shower, and put on some clothes. But before he did that he had to make sure she was okay, had to assure himself that whatever had threatened her was truly gone and had not simply made its way past him and turned back to finish whatever it had started.

Was the attacker someone after the formula Alice had discovered? And if so, was the goal to use or destroy it? It didn't matter. Danger was danger, no matter what the motive.

He thought he'd find Marnie in a panic, but she sat in a rocking chair on her back porch, a steaming cup of coffee in her hands. The woman did love her morning coffee. She still wore her robe, a fluffy blue monstrosity which was tightly belted, and her hair was nicely mussed. She wasn't wearing her glasses, or any makeup. He liked her this way. Raw. Natural. His. When she saw him she stood. He waited for panic, for a scream like the one that had alerted him that she was in danger.

She didn't scream. She didn't look at all worried or scared or disgusted.

Monster. Grotesque. He remembered the words she'd used to describe him. They still hurt.

She wasn't quite brave enough to leave the porch, but she did walk to the screen and look down at him. The screen was a fine mesh, but still obscured her face more than he liked. He took a few steps closer in order to see her more clearly, again expecting a frightened response from her. He didn't get one.

"Thank you," she said softly. Then she calmly took a sip of her coffee.

If he could answer in his current state he would, but words had never come to him in this form. There was only the whoop, and a growl, and the occasional grunt.

He could circle around and walk up her steps, though opening the screen door might be a problem. His hands were big and powerful, but they were not agile enough to grasp the tiny knob there. He could easily jump up, tear the screen away, and join her on the porch. She had to know that, and yet she did not seem concerned. Dyn Gwallt had the height and the strength, and she had no way of knowing that he was a peaceful creature, in this form more truly than in the other. Knowing that, seeing him up close and understanding his strength, Marnie didn't seem at all alarmed.

She placed one hand on the screen. The mesh gave a little at her touch. He reached up his own hand and barely touched it to hers. That insubstantial screen, which would be so easy to rip away, was the only thing between them. Even when his hand was there, touching hers, she did not move away.

"This is the weirdest town," she whispered. "I really should go. Coming here was a mistake. I could move in with my dad, for a while."

Clint couldn't help himself. He grunted.

Marnie dropped her hand. "As much as I hate to, I probably will. Or else I could stay with my friend in Birmingham for a while and look for a job there, though it wouldn't be in a library. I could find something else, I guess. But there's something I have to do first." She sighed and took another sip of coffee. "Somehow I have to get rid of a cryptozoologist."

Fresh out of the shower, Marnie dressed for a quiet Sunday. White capris. A blue blouse suitable for the heat. Tennis shoes. Like it or not, she might as well be prepared to run at a moment's notice. That seemed to be a requirement in this town.

She did wonder a time or two where Clint was, but deep down she knew. Something she'd said had spooked him big time, and he'd run. Literally. His clothes were draped over a chair in her bedroom. He hadn't even taken the time to dress, and he hadn't come back for them after his *run*.

Yeah, he'd run all right.

Only after she was dressed did she give the house a once over. The picture the shadowman had taken down remained in the dining room, leaning against the wall. There was no clear evidence of disturbance in the parlor, and yet... had that book been moved? Hadn't that ceramic cat been facing the window, not the door? A chair had been moved, judging by the indentation in the throw rug. Small things.

She probably should call the police, but after the way the chief had treated her last time she'd had a scare, she wasn't eager to contact him with this newest complaint. What was he going to do, anyway? He'd probably pat her on the head, call her little lady, and tell her it had all been her imagination. She'd spare herself that aggravation.

No, she had other, more important things on her mind. She wasn't going to stay in Mystic Springs, that was a given, but she couldn't leave town until she found a way to get rid of Nelson Lovell. Her email had brought him here, so he was her responsibility.

Bigfoot, or whatever it was, shouldn't be hunted like an animal. Even if it was an animal. Eye to eye contact and a touch of a, well, paw, and her mind had been changed. The beast was not a monster. It was not even a beast, not really. Bigfoot was a living creature with a heart. A warm and surely misunderstood being who had shown himself to her in order to save her from a shadow monster with a knife. Whatever it was, Bigfoot deserved to be left in peace.

The shadowy figure she'd found in her dining room scared her much more than Bigfoot ever could. Obviously the early morning light, or lack thereof, had played tricks on her mind and her eyes. She'd forgotten to lock the front door last night, or else Clint had not locked whatever door he'd exited for his late-night jog, and a thief had wandered in. A thief with a knife. A thief who had chased her out of her own house. Well, it wouldn't be her house much longer. Mystic Springs had been fun, but enough was enough. She'd get rid of Nelson and then she was gone.

What about Clint?

That question was a tough one. She liked him, she liked him a lot. The sex was great. He made her laugh, though he wasn't what anyone would call a funny guy. He made her forget all the weirdness in this crazy town. She'd really thought they had something special, something she'd been searching for her entire life. But he'd run out of her house naked in the middle of the night and not come back, so…

Marnie had to once again reevaluate her priorities. No, she didn't want Mr. Darcy, not anymore. She wanted someone real in her life. Someone warm and honest. She wanted to fall in love with a man she could trust and rely on, and she wanted him to love her. It didn't matter if he could say library properly, or if he was refined, or if he had a British accent or a waistcoat or a pretty face. She wanted a man who could love her, who could be her other half in all aspects of life.

Did such a creature exist? If there was really a Bigfoot, then maybe there was a chance.

She decided to walk to the B&B where Nelson had spent the night. It was a nice enough day, and after all the gumbo she'd eaten last night she could use the exercise. Janie was sitting on her front porch, shelling peas. Marnie waved, but didn't slow down. She had a purpose this morning. A plan, of sorts. When she reached Main Street she expected it to be empty, since all the businesses were closed on Sunday. At least, she thought they were. A number of people walked, as she did, toward the other end of town. Ah, it was Sunday, and there was a non-denominational church just down the road from the retirement village. Residents were walking to morning services. Among them, Felicity. The young girl wore her fair hair in her usual pigtails, but had traded in her shorts and t-shirt for a pretty dress made of a summer-light and flowery fabric.

Felicity turned back and ran a short distance to join Marnie. "Are you going to church? Mama will be so pleased."

"No, sorry. Perhaps another day. I'm on my way to see a friend."

Felicity scrunched up her nose. "The Bigfoot hunter."

"Yes. How did you know?"

A few of the people on the street turned to look at her. They weren't exactly friendly, but they didn't stare all that much, either. Maybe they were getting used to her. Too late.

"Everyone knows," Felicity said, spinning about on the sidewalk, doing a 360 that made her skirt float and her pigtails dance. "Clint must be so pis..." She stopped. "Annoyed. Clint must be annoyed."

"Why?" Good lord, did everyone in town know what was going on? And did they think Clint would be jealous of Nelson Lovell? "I barely know Nelson. And he won't be here very long, I'm sure." She intended to make sure of it.

"Good."

An attractive woman a block ahead turned and gave Felicity a frustrated wave.

"Gotta run! Maybe I'll see you later."

Run she did. Felicity was one of those children who was never still, who never walked when she could run or skip.

Marnie turned down the next street and walked toward the B&B at the far end of the road. If Nelson was a late sleeper, she might catch him in bed. He might be annoyed to be awakened. She didn't care. He had to go.

The B&B looked like many others. Old, white, square, three stories tall. The house might've been built a hundred years ago, or more. There were rose bushes galore around the wide front porch, and lace curtains in the windows. To the side was a gravel parking lot, where Nelson's ridiculous sports car was parked. Behind the B&B there was a well-tended lawn, but beyond that, woods. The entire town was surrounded by trees, all but isolating it.

If she could see into the forest well enough from her vantage point, she might be tempted – once more – to search for Bigfoot herself. She wasn't frightened of the creature the way she'd been just yesterday, when she'd hung back and let Nelson go into the woods alone.

She didn't want to hurt him, didn't even want a picture, as she had a few days ago. No, she wanted to apologize for bringing Nelson here. The creature who had chased away her shadowy intruder was gentle. He might not look it, but...

Truth was, she had a hundred questions for him.

Hmm. Him or her? With all that hair — long thick hair from head to toe — it had been impossible to tell. She hadn't point-edly looked, but at quick glance she hadn't noticed any genitalia. Still, she had sensed a masculine energy. And if Bigfoot was a woman, well, that would be unfortunate. Though logic dictated...

Logic? Who was she kidding? And from all she could tell, Bigfoot wasn't capable of answering any questions, not from her or anyone else.

Nelson was not still asleep; he sat alone at the long table in the B&B dining room, sipping at a fine china cup filled with steaming coffee, or perhaps tea, and picking at what was left of a muffin. No one else was present, not another guest, an employee, or the owner. The room looked as if it hadn't changed in a hundred years. The polished wooden table could easily seat a dozen, but it was set, on this Sunday morning, for one. The chairs appeared to be old and unsubstantial — the legs were spindly — but like the table they were polished and elegant. The rug was worn but not shabby, and the dark wooden floors beneath were clean and shiny, with only the occasional hint of warping.

The only thing in the room that was out of place was the man at the table. Nelson didn't belong here. With his weirdly fancy clothes and his man bun, with his obvious disdain, he did not belong.

She could empathize. It was a lonely feeling to be out of step, to not fit in.

Marnie had never truly trusted her instincts. For a long time, she hadn't believed she had any. At the very least, those instincts hadn't been what anyone would call sharp. But standing in the doorway of this finely furnished room, she experienced a rush of knowledge, a certainty, that she should not have sent that email.

Nelson turned his head, smiled at her, and then he winked. "You look lovely this morning," he said, as if he hadn't told her yesterday that the camera added ten pounds.

"Thanks," she said. "Look, I have a confession to make." She took a deep breath and steeled her spine.

He stood slowly and indicated the chair beside him. "Join me for tea while we talk about our plans for the day."

Marnie did her best to be tough. Nothing else would do, in this circumstance. "We have no plans for the day. I'm afraid I've wasted your time. I was obviously suffering from heat exhaustion and hallucinating when I saw what I thought I saw, and I…"

His smile faded, his eyes narrowed. For an instant he was not so pretty; he was not pretty at all. "You're having second thoughts."

"Well…" Marnie squirmed. This was not fun, nor was it easy. "Yes. I didn't intentionally lie, but the more I think about that day the more I wonder. You see, I had a terrible time getting here. There was a flat tire, and it was so hot, and I had to walk the road in heels." She dipped her head then peeked up at Nelson. "Maybe I had a panic attack."

She expected him to be angry. After all, she'd wasted his time. She saw that anger in his expression, but then it faded. He resumed his seat, took a sip of tea, then said — eyes straight ahead, not on her at all, "I don't believe you. I don't know why you're trying to take back what you said to me, but I can see it all too well. You're a terrible liar."

"I'm actually a very good…" She stopped abruptly.

Nelson looked at her once more, his eyes calculating. "What made you change your mind? Why are you trying to get rid of me?"

"I'm not trying to get rid of you," Marnie said, hoping she was a better liar than he gave her credit for. "You're welcome to stay in Mystic Springs as long as you'd like." She was confident that if there was no Bigfoot, he'd blow out of this town in a heartbeat. Nothing else here would interest him.

"If I decide to stay, will you continue to assist me?"

After a brief hesitation, Marnie shook her head.

"Why, I wonder?" he asked. "What's changed in a day?"

I met the monster and he is not a monster after all. She couldn't tell him that.

Elaine Forrester saved her from having to come up with a response. The hefty woman, wearing a bright yellow dress that appeared to be almost as old as the house, swept into the room with flair, a smile on her face, her white hair flowing behind her. Marnie had met Elaine briefly at the reception Friday evening, but knew little about her. What she did know at a glance was that the older woman was smitten with her houseguest.

Nelson stood, smiled at the B&B owner, then took her hand in his and kissed it. "Mrs. Forrester, you are a vision, as always."

The woman giggled like a girl. "Oh, dear, how many times do I have to tell you to call me Elaine?"

A shiver walked up Marnie's spine. The British accent, the charming smile, the compliments, the way Nelson had of looking a woman in the eye as he spoke. Good Lord, he was like a cobra.

When was he going to strike?

Clint stood on the sidewalk in front of Marnie's house, staring at the door. She wasn't inside. He knew it, felt it, smelled it. Where was she? Out with Lovell, he imagined, looking for proof that Bigfoot existed. Looking for him.

He shouldn't be surprised. He hadn't known Marnie Somerset a week. She was pretty and funny and great in bed, but he didn't know her. It had been foolish to think he did, to imagine for a while that they might have something.

They'd see her out of town with a cup of amnesia punch, as they did all Non-Springers who saw more of Mystic Springs than they should. At least Frannie had promised not to make another cake for the new librarian. Bizarre and potentially deadly as she was, Frannie was a woman of her word.

Marnie deserved better. After all, when she'd brought his greatest nightmare to his door she hadn't realized who — what — he was.

And still, he felt as betrayed as he had when he'd discovered that Jenna had spent years trying to find a way to fix him.

He didn't want to be fixed. He certainly didn't want to be a part of Lovell's damn TV show.

Maybe it was time to give up the fantasy that he might find a woman to call his own, that he might one day have what his parents had found. A forever partner. Someone who would love and accept him as he was.

He glanced to the house next door, as James Garvin stepped onto his front porch. Clint raised a hand in a half-hearted wave; the grumpy old man did not return that greeting.

Now would be a perfect time to search the house for the formula Susan had asked him to find. It didn't matter that Garvin was watching. Didn't matter if anyone else had seen him, either. If he was caught inside the house with Marnie not at home, it would be easy enough to explain why he was there. They were sleeping together, after all.

Or had been.

"Hi."

Clint nearly jumped out of his skin. No one snuck up on him!

He should've heard Marnie coming for a block, or more. He should've smelled her.

He smelled her now. She smelled of coffee and cinnamon, of old books and new, of Marnie. And she smelled a little of Nelson Lovell.

She sighed. "We need to talk."

CHAPTER 16

THEY'D NEVER SAT in the parlor to visit, like a normal couple might. No, she and Clint had spent their time together in the bedroom, and the kitchen, and in the bedroom again. She wanted to have this particular conversation here; she on the sofa, Clint in a man-sized chair that faced her.

She needed a bit of physical distance. When it came to Clint, she was far too easily distracted. If he touched her, all bets were off.

"Have you ever seen anything odd in Mystic Springs?" she asked. "Around town, maybe in the woods."

"Your Bigfoot," Clint clarified for her. He didn't exactly snap at her, but his voice was so terse he came close.

Marnie nodded. He didn't answer, so she continued. "I made a terrible mistake, contacting Nelson. I told him I must've been hallucinating, that I hadn't really seen anything at all, but he didn't buy it."

Clint's eyebrows rose a little. "You really did try to get rid of him?"

She nodded again.

"Why?"

Marnie pursed her lips. This was harder than she'd imagined it would be.

With Jay, and with previous boyfriends, she'd always kept a part of herself at a distance. She understood that, now. She'd liked them all, some more than others, and there had been rare moments with each of them that made her hope for more, that made her hope for trust.

She did not share all of herself; she never had. Her thoughts, her fears, her indecisions. They were for her alone, and always had been. Maybe that was a reaction to her parents' bad marriage and all that had followed. Her mother had chosen a man over her kids. Her father believed in love at first sight, and fell in and out of love quickly and completely. Maybe watching them and their mistakes made her more cautious than she needed to be. Maybe she'd never truly trusted anyone.

Until now. She wanted to tell Clint everything.

"It sounds crazy." Maybe she wasn't ready, even now. "I don't want you to think I'm a complete nutcase."

"What if I said yes, I've seen what you said you saw. Then what?"

Relief washed through her; she closed her eyes and sighed. "Thank God. There were times I thought I had lost my mind."

"And if you haven't?"

How much could she share? She didn't think Clint would be like Nelson, she didn't think he'd harm her Bigfoot. Yes, the creature was hers, in a weird way. But still, could she trust anyone?

What choice did she have? If she was ever going to open up to a man, Clint was — could be — might be — the one.

"This morning, I looked into Bigfoot's eyes," she said. "I saw more than hair and huge hands and feet. I saw more than his size and strength. He's not a monster, and he doesn't deserve to be hunted by a man like Nelson Lovell. Or anyone else, but especially not that snake."

"I thought you liked Lovell."

"I did, for about half an hour," she admitted. "Do you know, he told me, *while I was eating*, that the camera adds ten pounds? He could've at least waited until I'd finished my chicken pot pie." He'd also said she could do better where men were concerned, but she saw no reason to share that tidbit with Clint. If he took it the wrong way, Nelson might have more to worry about than his search for Bigfoot. Though if she told all, she'd have help running Nelson out of town. That wouldn't be a bad thing.

No, this was her mess, and she needed to be the one to fix it. It would be so easy for her to lean on Clint, to ask him to help her, to play the damsel in distress. In all honesty she'd fallen for him too easily and too fast. She'd let herself be sucked in by his rustic charm and his good looks, the same way she'd let herself be fooled – though not for long – by an English accent and a brocade vest.

She should've instantly known not to trust a man who wore a vest in the summertime in Alabama.

"I've made so many mistakes," she whispered.

"Am I one of those mistakes?" Clint asked, without anger, without even much curiosity.

She hesitated, but not for long. "Yes, I think so." He didn't feel like a mistake, not really, but she'd been in Mystic Springs less than a week and already he felt necessary, as if he were a part of her. That couldn't be natural. It couldn't be right. She didn't want to be like her dad, who loved so quickly and then was always hurt in the end. The women he loved were always hurt, too. "I need some time to myself."

"How much time?"

"I don't know."

Clint stood slowly. If he came toward her, if he kissed her, if he touched her, she'd crumble. She'd give in. She'd throw aside all caution to have him. That wasn't right, it wasn't wise. Had she ever been wise? Was it too late to start?

"Let me get your clothes," she said, spinning on her heel and all but running from Clint. She needed a moment to breathe, to gather her strength. It would be too easy to fall into his arms again. She needed to be strong, needed to stand on her own two feet. Besides, it wasn't like she planned to stay in Mystic Springs much longer. Her adventure, her new beginning, it was a mistake. It was already time to move on and leave this weirdness behind.

Including Clint.

She returned to the parlor with his clothes, neatly folded, shoes on top, in hand. He didn't come forward to meet her, not even with one small step. Marnie handed his things over, managing to do so without brushing his hands with hers. It helped that he seemed as reluctant for skin to skin contact as she was.

She was both relieved and disappointed when he nodded once and headed for the front door.

Clint walked toward home at a fast pace. Shit. Things had been so simple before Marnie Somerset had come to town. She stirred him up, made him consider impossible things, distracted him from work and his hard-won belief that he needed nothing and no one.

Now there was Lovell to take care of. And how the hell was he supposed to keep an eye on Marnie if she wanted to be alone? How was he supposed to search for Alice's formula if Marnie wouldn't let him in the house?

The situation with Lovell was annoying, but taking care of the cryptozoologist would be easy enough. Even though he'd love to find a permanent way to get rid of Lovell, amnesia punch was the way to go. People disappearing for good always raised more of a stink than a few bad memories. Or a big hole in the memory.

Mystic Springs could be erased from Lovell's memory, with a cup of punch from Ivy's hands. Susan was great with electronics. She could make Marnie's emails to the Bigfoot hunter disappear, as well as any Lovell had sent to others. It would've been easier if Lovell had accepted Marnie's insistence that she hadn't seen Bigfoot after all, but it didn't sound as if that was going to work.

It could be done.

Marnie presented a more complicated problem. They needed her, or so Luke said. She was living in a house where the formula necessary to remove Mystic Springs from the map was most likely hidden. More than one someone wanted that formula, and there was no telling what they'd do to get it.

Someone had killed Alice for it.

Marnie had ordered him out of her life and her house, in a very polite, firm, and hesitant way. If she stayed, maybe eventually he'd end up back in her good graces, and back in her bed. But he wouldn't push her, wouldn't try to charm her into picking up where they left off. She had doubts. She was allowed.

As Clint turned through a thick stand of trees and approached his front porch, another thought came to him. A memory of his own. *He doesn't deserve to be hunted by a man like Nelson Lovell.* And then: *Somehow I have to get rid of a cryptozoologist.*

Maybe Marnie did need some time alone, but this wasn't over. Not by a long shot.

Nelson called his camera crew Sunday afternoon and instructed them to hold off. He explained that he was less certain about the Mystic Springs story than he'd initially been. He told them he wanted to do more investigating before bringing them in, because he didn't want to waste their time.

In normal circumstances, he would've left town the minute a so-called witness backed off their story. It happened all the time. Someone would spin a story for the attention, for the fun of it, and they were always found out. He didn't waste his time chasing ghosts or placating crackpots.

But this time he would stay as long as it took. Something about this place was off. He'd been here for twenty-four hours, and already he was different. This place affected him, somehow. Last night, as he'd lay in a too-soft bed with a white canopy, he'd noticed a number of smells. At first he'd written it off to the odors in this creepy old house. Mold and food and the old lady's perfume. But after a while, he'd found himself able to identify the odors.

Roses from the garden. Bacon the old lady had cooked that morning. A chicken from two or three days before. He was a vegan! Perhaps not an entirely dedicated one, but he had not eaten meat in three years.

Lying in bed, smelling chicken and bacon, he wanted meat. Lots of it.

Instead of raiding the kitchen, he concentrated on other smells. Not just from the house, he realized, but from well beyond.

He could smell the river, the fish in it, the faint odor of a chemical that floated by. He caught a hint of the aroma of bread being baked, an aroma that came not from this house but from another somewhere nearby. Maybe not so nearby.

Nelson heard small movements from downstairs, and if he put forth an effort he could even hear small animals rustling leaves in the woods behind this B&B. Children playing down the street. The ordinary creaks and pops any old house might make.

Those creaks and pops made him jump a bit, they were so loud. Eventually he was able to tune them out, but it was definitely odd.

After he hung up on his producer, Nelson walked to the window of his second-story room and looked out on a well-manicured yard. There were flowers everywhere, and a small vegetable garden, but there was also lots of very green grass.

Running was not his thing — he didn't like to sweat — but at the moment he wanted nothing more than to run across that yard. He wanted to rip off his clothes, jump from this window, and run until he couldn't run anymore.

He didn't do any of those things, but instead walked down the stairs and out the front door. It was time to explore Mystic Springs. Something odd was going on here, and he intended to find out what it was.

By the time Sunday evening rolled around, Marnie was second guessing her decision to cool things with Clint. The fact that she didn't like being alone had something to do with it, she reasoned. She couldn't shake — would never shake — the memory of the shadowman who'd broken into her house. Try as she might, she could not convince herself that the shadow had been a delusion.

The easiest thing to do would be to send the town council an email of resignation, load up her car as best she could, and leave Mystic Springs like the devil was on her heels. That was her natural instinct, to run away.

She hadn't *literally* run away since that summer she'd turned twelve. And she'd been gone such a short amount of time, no one but Marnie knew she'd packed a backpack and walked a full three blocks before turning around and heading home.

That had been the summer her parents divorced. She'd been positive they'd be so sorry she was gone they'd stay together. Only a naive child would think that way.

She was no longer a child, and while she might be naive on occasion, she'd like to think she was a discerning adult.

A creepy-looking, oddly-disguised someone breaking into her house was important. She had the distinct feeling her life had been in danger, and that definitely qualified. Was that enough to make her run? Maybe. She sensed, in a way she could not explain, that Clint could be important. Enough to entice her to stay? Again, maybe.

Leftover gumbo served as supper. Damn, Clint was handsome, a successful writer, and a pretty darn good cook to boot. She added great in the sack to the list of his attributes. Dammit, she missed him. She missed him much more than she should, considering how long she'd known him.

All that aside, she needed time to think, and with Clint around she didn't. She didn't think at all. When he was with her, all she did was feel.

Logic had never been her strong suit, at least not when it came to men. That needed to change. She had to quit leaping into relationships without a moment of critical thought.

There were other reasons to stay, she decided, calling upon the logical Marnie that didn't always show up when she was needed. The library was fantastic, perhaps the best she'd ever seen. It was definitely the best she'd ever worked in, and it was hers, all hers. The people in town were certainly odd, but there were a handful that might one day be friends. Gabi. Eve. Susan. The charming Felicity. She would love to win over the grumpy Ivy. Anyone who could bake like Ivy could had to have a good side.

And then there was — she had to say it, if not out loud then to herself — Bigfoot. The creature that had initially frightened her had turned out to be entirely different than she'd imagined. Gentler. Not a beast, not a monster at all. Her Bigfoot was hairy beyond belief, large and strong and yes, a little smelly, but not a monster.

She wanted to know more. She wanted to see it — him — again. She really wanted to give him a name of some kind, something other than Bigfoot. From all she'd gathered he couldn't tell her his name, or anything else, and to just label him with her own choice would be like naming a dog. He was no one's pet.

If she spoke would he understand her? Could he communicate with her at all?

No more emails to Bigfoot hunters. No more research. Marnie wanted to discover more about Bigfoot all on her own. She just wasn't sure how to go about it.

She shouldn't feel safe in this house. The shadowman had invaded it, had broken in with ill intent. She was as alone as she'd ever been, with no one in shouting distance. Since Clint had left she'd kept her cell phone close at hand. If she dialed 9-1-1 who would answer? Police Chief Benedict, she imagined. He wouldn't take her seriously, she knew it. She was unlikely to find any real help there.

After a while she set the cell phone aside. She only picked it up once to send a quick text to Chelsea.

Can I stay with you for a couple of days if I need to?

Chelsea, who was never far from her cell, answered quickly. *Of course. Is everything OK?*

Was everything okay? No, it was not. But Marnie answered. *Everything's fine, just not sure the job is going to work out.* That was an understatement, but there was no way she could tell Chelsea what was going on in a text. Maybe in person, after at least one bottle of wine. Each.

Chelsea answered with a thumbs up emoji.

So, that was a plan. If she had to run, she knew where she'd be running to.

Marnie cleaned the kitchen, picked out an outfit to wear to work tomorrow, and emailed her mother. She lied and said that all was well. As she took care of these normal chores, a calmness seemed to work through her. Everything would be okay, somehow. Maybe Clint would be a part of that okay, and maybe he would not, but she would survive this.

Her job in the small town with the fabulous library had turned into an adventure after all. Doors and windows locked, bedroom closets checked — just in case — Marnie climbed into bed with a sigh and a smile.

CHAPTER 17

ON MONDAY MORNING, a few people came into the library. Some of them checked out books, while others browsed aimlessly. The browsers spent most of their time checking out the new librarian. Marnie was as friendly as she could be, smiling, offering to help in any way she could. By lunchtime, she was optimistic about the health of the Mystic Springs Library.

She walked across the street to Eve's for lunch, intending to grab a salad. As had become the norm, she passed on the salad and went for the daily special. Red beans and rice with lots of spicy sausage. It was fantastic.

Halfway through her meal, she looked up to see a surprisingly disheveled Nelson Lovell approaching her booth. His hair was loose and tangled. He wore jeans and a blue short sleeved shirt that was incorrectly buttoned. No waistcoat today. He glanced this way and that, as if he were looking for someone, before sitting down across from Marnie.

"I thought you'd be gone by now," she said, in a less than kind voice.

He seemed not to notice her tone. "No. Can't. Something is wrong with me."

Had his British accent faded? It definitely sounded different today.

Eve approached with an order pad in hand. "Another salad?" she asked, a bite in her voice.

Nelson shook his head. "No, no, I'll have a hamburger, rare. Make that two. I'm starving."

Eve pursed her lips, muttered, "Okay," and walked away.

Marnie had almost finished her red beans and rice. She was beyond full, but it was too good to leave behind. Nelson pointed, shaking one long finger at her lunch, and asked, "Are you going to finish that?" Before she could answer, he pulled the bowl across the table and began to eat. He didn't even bother to ask for a clean spoon, just took hers and dug in.

Marnie leaned back, took a sip of her iced tea, and studied Nelson. Two days ago he'd been a refined vegan with a crisp British accent, a man bun, and a stylish way of dressing. Today he was entirely changed.

Mystic Springs could do that to a person.

"What happened to your accent?" she asked as he shoveled a big spoonful of beans and rice into his mouth.

He stopped chewing for a moment, swallowed, then looked her in the eye. "Nothing," he said. "My accent is as it has always been." And for that moment, it was.

"I thought you were a vegan," she said, leaning slightly forward.

"How can I remain a vegan when meat smells so damned magnificent?" He scraped the bowl with her spoon — his spoon now — and downed the last of the red beans and rice just as Eve approached with his burgers.

Before Eve could make her getaway, Nelson reached out and gripped her wrist. Eve was visibly startled; Nelson wisely released her. "Milkshake. Do you have milkshakes? I want one. Chocolate."

"Coming right up." She leaned down and whispered, "Don't touch me again, or you'll be eating your burgers one-handed."

He nodded, unfazed by the threat. His focus was entirely on the food before him.

Marnie was finished with her lunch; she couldn't eat another bite. She really should pay and get back to work, but this was fascinating. She'd been impulsive herself, since coming to this odd town, but she wasn't nearly as changed as Nelson was. He had become an entirely different person.

She wasn't going to get any information out of him before he finished his meal, so as Eve approached with his milkshake, Marnie stood and said, "Come over to the library when you're finished with lunch."

He muttered what seemed to be an agreement, though she couldn't be sure he understood a word she said.

Feeling wonderfully full and all but drunk, though he couldn't remember the last time he'd consumed alcohol, Nelson crossed the street to the library. He looked inside and saw Marnie talking to a little girl with pigtails. If the librarian who'd brought him to this town looked up she'd see him standing there, on the other side of the glass door, but she didn't look up. She smiled. She laughed.

She'd lied to him.

He'd crossed the street with every intention of walking through that door to ask Marnie why she'd asked him to come to the library, but instead he turned away, walking, walking, then running toward the end of the street and the woods beyond. They smelled so good, each leaf its own perfume. The forest called to him, beckoned him into its arms.

Nelson had awakened that morning itching and hungry and somehow angry. He'd dressed quickly and gone downstairs to devour his breakfast, ignoring the annoying old woman who had prepared it. No longer hungry but still so antsy he could not possibly sit still, he'd burst through the B&B back door to run through the yard to the woods beyond.

Running was glorious.

He'd been fascinated by Bigfoot since he'd been a boy. From Texas, to Oregon, to Florida, he'd searched. The fake accent and doctored background had come later, when he'd decided to make his passion a career.

No one would take Nelson Lovell — An embarrassing Nelly to family — steel worker's son, seriously.

So he'd left home and started exploring. He'd changed his way of dressing and his voice, and he'd let his hair grow long. He'd created a fictional backstory for Nelson Lovell, and had charmed his way into the life he wanted. He'd always been a charmer, had been able to snow teachers, women, debt collectors…

He should've been an actor.

Nelson hadn't spoken to his father in years. His mother was long gone, and his brothers… hell, he had no idea where they were. When he made a new life he didn't do it in half measures. He embraced it. He'd left everything and everyone of Nelly behind. This was not a part of the plan.

Deeper and deeper into the woods he went. He ran between trees, leapt over a bush that was in his path, and bathed himself in the smells and sounds of the forest. They were so acute, they blinded him to everything else. There was just this, just the trees and the small creatures, and the drive to run.

He tripped over the root of a tree that jutted up above the path. Grace had never been his strong suit; he worked very hard to present an air of easy confidence and strength. Still, rarely did he lose his balance this way. He stumbled and tried to recover but could not. He scraped his cheek on the hard ground as he gave into the fall, and even that was wonderful. Bloody brilliant, he might've said if anyone was listening.

Nelson didn't immediately rise, but rolled onto his back and took a few deep breaths. On his back on the ground, he stared up at the sky beyond the trees. He began to unbutton his shirt, not sure why, really. The sensation of clothing against his skin was annoying; that was reason enough. A strange tingle worked its way up his spine. It hurt. It was wonderful. It was frightening.

He lifted his hand, which had begun to itch, and watched as a number of long, dark hairs pushed their way beyond the skin and quickly grew to a length of five inches, or more. He felt the same sensation on one side of his face, and on his legs. Even his ass itched.

He quickly shimmied his pants and boxers down and off, kicking off his boots as he whipped the jeans from his body. Nelson lay naked in the forest, part human, part hairy creature. One leg was completely hairy; the other was misshapen and had tufts of dark hair here and there. He should be alarmed, but instead he laughed. Damn, he felt good.

After a long, quiet moment he stood, studying his body as best he could. He longed for a mirror, but a look down would have to do for now. The hair, the muscles, the immense size of his hands and feet... *hairy* hands and feet...

"What am I?" he tried to whisper, but what came out was a garbled mess of unintelligible words.

He should be horrified, but he was not. Following his new instincts he climbed the nearest tree with incredible ease. When he reached the top he gave an instinctive, joyous "Whoop!" that reverberated through the woods.

Clint had been trying to write, but hadn't gotten far. The story wasn't working. His mind wandered. Normally he had no trouble concentrating when he was at the computer, but today was a different story. He'd been yawning since he got started, which didn't help matters at all.

It should be no surprise that he was exhausted. He'd spent half the night prowling around Marnie's house, making sure she was safe, making sure no one saw his absence as an opportunity to break in. He didn't care if the intention was to search for the formula, scare her out of town, or physically harm her, he would protect her from it all.

He'd never had the urge to protect anyone before, not like this.

The startling call from the forest made his hair stand on end. Clint leapt from his chair, straining to listen. Was his imagination working overtime? What the hell? That was his sound, his alone. There were no other Dyn Gwallts in or around Mystic Springs. At least, there shouldn't be.

But that sound, it had not been his imagination.

He left his computer behind and headed for the deck, stripping as he walked. Once he was outdoors, he lifted his head and took a long, deep breath. What struck him, what he inhaled, was the odor of another of his kind, mingled with the stink of a man he had come to despise.

"Shit," he tried to say, as he leapt over the deck railing and onto the ground, ignoring the pain of the change. The resulting growl sent birds and small creatures scattering in all directions.

He ran, guided by smell, intrigued and alarmed at the same time, until he came across an area where the scent was so strong it stopped him in his tracks. He looked up and there it was, high in a pine tree.

Half man, half Dyn Gwallt, Nelson Lovell leaned forward and whooped again.

Was this what he looked like in the midst of a shift? It was grotesque, to be caught in between. There were tufts of hair in some places and patches of smooth, pale skin in others. Lovell's face was barely recognizable. It was twisted, neither human nor

Dyn Gwallt. One leg, the hairiest one, was significantly longer than the other.

Lovell leaned forward. Clint growled a warning. The Bigfoot hunter — and how ironic was that? — was too far up. The fall would be...

It happened fast. Lovell didn't fall, he jumped. Clint moved out of the way, as the beast landed. The more human leg took the brunt of it, buckling under, bending back in a sickeningly unnatural way. In pain, the creature screamed. The sound that came from a misshapen mouth was a garbled mess of sounds at first, but soon changed to a very human scream as Lovell shifted entirely into his human form.

The scream of pain changed to one of terror as he looked up at Clint, as he looked up into the face of the Bigfoot he had hunted for so long.

"Son of a fucking bitch!" Lovell screamed, without a trace of a British accent.

Marnie walked home from work, after a satisfying day. Well, satisfying in the librarian sense. Several people had stopped by, including Felicity. They'd had a very nice conversation, about books and ice cream, the ice cream shop Marnie had yet to visit, and the best treats from Ivy's.

She hadn't seen Clint, which disappointed her even though she'd been the one to tell him they needed time apart. At least, *she* needed time.

Looking forward to kicking off her shoes and heating up the last of the gumbo, Marnie was surprised — and a little disappointed — to see Elaine Forrester sitting on her front porch. She really was tired, and not inclined to indulge in idle chitchat at the moment. The owner of the B&B held a cloth-covered wicker basket on her lap; she smiled widely as Marnie approached.

"I seem to have lost my boarder," she said in a cheery voice. "Have you seen him?"

"Nelson Lovell?"

Elaine's eyes seem to harden. One of them narrowed slightly. "He's the only boarder I have, at the moment."

Marnie climbed the steps. "I saw him at lunchtime. He was supposed to stop by the library after he finished eating, but did not." Talking about Nelson made her wonder, again, what had happened to him. "Maybe he left town. I think his work here is done." It should be.

Elaine didn't accept that explanation. "Why would he leave without taking his clothes, his computer, his cell phone? And that fancy car of his is right where he left it."

It would be easy enough to notice that the car was still there, but what about the rest? Had the old woman searched Nelson's room or had she simply seen his things as she'd made the bed? She did seem a bit like a snooper. "I wouldn't worry."

"You're right. He's a grown man and will show up when he feels like it. I'm such a worrywart." Elaine stood. "I brought you a little something for supper." She lifted the pale pink cloth to reveal what was beneath. "Chicken salad sandwiches, my famous vegetable soup, and a double fudge brownie."

Marnie could almost groan. She'd eaten far too well in the past week. Any day now, her clothes were going to start getting tighter. It usually started in the hips. But she just smiled, thanked Elaine, and unlocked the front door hoping the B&B owner would head for home, with the meal delivered and her question about Nelson answered.

Instead, the older woman continued to chat, following Marnie into the house and then to the kitchen, where Marnie placed the basket on the table. "I'll dig into this later. Thank you so much."

Elaine took a seat at the table. "Do try my soup. It's famous around these parts. I grow my own herbs." She reached into the basket and pulled out a small glass bowl with a dark blue lid. "It's still warm, see? I love to see the expressions on people's faces when they eat the food I prepared. It's my greatest joy."

Taking a deep breath, Marnie fetched a spoon from the silverware drawer and sat across the table from Elaine. She'd rather have leftover gumbo, but it seemed the only way she was going to get rid of the woman was to eat the damn soup. She removed the lid and spooned a bit into her mouth. Okay, so it was good. Very good. Maybe not Eve-good or gumbo-good, but she liked it. Another spoonful followed the first, and then another, and then another, until the small bowl was empty.

"You're such a good girl," Elaine said in a soothing voice.

Marnie tried to stand, intending to put her bowl and spoon into the sink, but she had a bout of lightheadedness that caused her to sit down. Hard. The room swam. "Goodness, I have no idea why I'm so dizzy." Her words were oddly slurred. She tried again to get up and could not. Okay, it had been a long day and she was pretty tired, but this was ridiculous.

Elaine patted her hand, then took the bowl and spoon. She didn't just place them in the sink, she washed both thoroughly then returned the spoon to its place in the drawer and the bowl to her basket.

The edges of her world were going dim, but Marnie heard Elaine well enough as she said, "Now you sit right here while we take a look around. We don't want to have to kill you, if we don't have to. Alice didn't believe us when we told her that, and now look where she is. Stubborn old witch," she muttered under her breath.

We?

When Marnie shuddered, Elaine gently took her head and placed it on the table, right before everything went black.

CHAPTER 18

As luck would have it — bad luck — Lovell's leg was broken. If he'd been fully transformed that never would've happened, but his shift had remained incomplete.

The cryptozoologist was sleeping — passed out, more likely — on Clint's den sofa, with a crocheted afghan draped over his still-naked body. Clint had run home with the wounded Lovell draped over his shoulder, deposited the man on the couch, shifted and dressed. Now he watched.

He'd be happy to loan the man a change of clothes, but he wasn't about to dress him in his sleep, or whatever this was.

Clint sat in a recliner a few feet away, eyes on Lovell's tortured face.

Obviously Lovell had Springer blood. Maybe he was a distant cousin, though it was possible he'd descended from an entirely different bloodline. No one had bothered to write down the history of his kind, at least, not that he knew of. Were there others out there? Of course there were.

Nelson Lovell been born in the world, far away from Mystic Springs, but the minute he'd come to town his magic had begun to awaken.

Amnesia punch didn't always work on a Springer. It was iffy, at best. Funeral cake? Who knew? It had been more than fifty years since that method had been used, or so he heard. Still, Frannie managed to bake one when she felt the need, as she had for Marnie. The cake was always fatal. Anyone who consumed it would be dead within a matter of days, but not by any kind of poison. They might be hit by a car, have a heart attack, trip and fall down the stairs.

In the old days Springers might've been inclined to take care of their problems in such a manner, but these days they didn't make a habit of killing one another, if they could help it. Frannie was getting old. Clint hoped the recipe died with her.

Something would have to be done. They couldn't have the Bigfoot hunter going back into the world to tell people that he himself was Bigfoot. If the man had any self-preservation instincts at all, he'd keep their secret. They all did, had always done. But there was no guarantee Lovell had even a lick of common sense, so...

What the hell were they going to do with him?

Lovell came awake slowly, tossing on the couch, his expression one of pain. One eye opened, then another. He looked at Clint, jumped a little, and tried to get up. He didn't get far before flinching. "Why am I here?" He lifted the blanket and peered beneath. "And why am I naked?"

If he didn't remember...

Judging by the dawning expression on Lovell's face, he remembered everything. "Bloody hell..."

"You can drop the phony accent," Clint said.

He did, without argument. "I think I broke my leg."

"Likely," Clint said without concern.

"Is there a doctor in this godforsaken town?"

"We have a vet."

Lovell leaned back and sighed. "I suppose that's appropriate."

He was taking this better than Clint had imagined he would, so far.

"You won't need him," Clint said. "The leg will heal quickly." That process had already started, deep in the bone. The healing would progress quickly from there.

Lovell didn't question that statement, as he should've. Instead he looked Clint over critically, one eye narrowed as he pushed a long lock of hair away from his face. "Are you..."

"Depends," Clint snapped. "Is this going in one of your damn books?"

A shrug, a roll of the eyes. "No one would believe me," Lovell said calmly.

"If I say yes?"

Lovell sat up. If he was still in pain, he didn't let it show. "I want to know everything. From the beginning. I want the complete story of this place, the reason I am what I am and you are what you are. Why now? And why am I so hungry?"

Clint stood. "I'll get you some clothes and a sandwich, and then we'll talk."

"Two!" Lovell called out as Clint walked away.

Clint stopped and turned. "Two what?"

"Two sandwiches. I'm starving."

Marnie opened one eye and then the other. Oh my God, what a headache! But she was alive, at least. That crazy old woman hadn't killed her. Yet.

She was still at the kitchen table, but now her hands were tied behind her back and she was lashed to the chair with one of her own scarves. Judging by the light from the single window, only an hour or two had passed since she'd eaten that damned soup. There was still plenty of light in the sky on this long summer day.

She lifted her head and looked around. Holy shit! It looked as if a tornado had blown through her kitchen. The cabinets had been emptied, and so had the fridge. The garbage can was on its side, contents spilled onto the floor; the sugar canister had been emptied onto the counter.

Elaine wasn't in the room, though it was obvious she'd been busy here for a while. What a mess! Marnie heard a noise, the thud of a heavy item of some kind being dropped, it sounded like. At a distance, perhaps from the parlor, something hit the floor and broke with a crash. A piece of furniture was moved; legs scraped across a wooden floor.

And a man's gravelly voice said, "The formula has to be some-where else. Let's just burn this place to the ground and be done with it."

Elaine made what seemed to be a soft argument — at least Marnie hoped it was an argument — and the man, whoever he was, scoffed and cursed.

When she heard footsteps headed her way, Marnie placed her head back on the table and closed her eyes. Maybe they'd think she was still out. Maybe they'd just leave.

Yeah, right.

"You can't fool me, dear," Elaine said in a cheery voice. "Open those eyes and let's have a talk."

Marnie opened her eyes and lifted her head. If she remained calm, maybe she'd get out of this alive. If she played along, maybe they wouldn't hurt her. "What are you looking for? Maybe I can help."

"You wouldn't understand," Elaine said in a condescending tone.

"Try me."

A man who appeared to be north of eighty walked into the kitchen. After a moment Marnie realized that she'd seen him before, in Eve's and on the front porch of the house next door.

She'd waved. He'd ignored her, then retreated into his house, slamming the door behind him.

Her grumpy neighbor was the one who wanted to burn this house down. With her in it.

"We're looking for something the previous resident of this house hid from us. It must be destroyed before the wrong people find it."

"What is it?"

"A spell, I guess you might say. That's not entirely correct but as a Non-Springer you're not likely to understand the nuances of such a powerful magic."

Magic? *Spell?*

Elaine continued, "The previous librarian concocted a formula to go along with a spell, and she was just about to put it into action when James here removed her from this world." She cast a censuring glance at the man who stood behind her. "Prematurely, as we can't be sure where she hid the formula, and it's important that we confirm it's been destroyed." She looked around the kitchen she'd searched so thoroughly. "Alice loved this house. I do so hate to burn it, at least until we can be certain the spell is hidden here."

"Wait a minute," Marnie said, squirming. Her brain was processing a lot of information at the moment, but one detail stood out. "This was the old librarian's house? And she was murdered here?"

James grinned. "Yep. We were having a nice talk right here in this kitchen. She figured out what was what and tried to run. I grabbed her iron skillet off the stove and chased her to the front of the house. Lucky for me, my friend here was standing in the doorway, so Alice ran into the front bedroom and tried to lock the door. She was too slow. I bashed her across the head with her own iron skillet." He leaned forward. "Three times, to be sure the job was done."

"That's... you... I can't..."

The old man flicked a finger in Marnie's direction, and her words were silenced. She tried to speak, she made the effort, but no words came out.

"James, really," Elaine said gently.

"She was sputtering. I can't stand that. She can still listen."

Marnie pursed her lips together and glared, as best she could, at the man who wanted to burn her house. He'd killed here before and would not hesitate to do so again. She tried to speak, but nothing happened. Reluctantly, James flicked his fingers and her words returned. "Why?" she asked. "What does this spell do?"

"Alice and a few others wanted to remove this town from the map, to hide us from the rest of the world. It's a world that doesn't accept us, that doesn't suit us, so I can see the appeal in the idea. If she had succeeded, and she almost did, no one would come in ever again, and no one would leave. Mystic Springs would become a prison, of sorts, though of course Alice didn't see it that way. Why should we be punished for being who we are? Why should we be imprisoned here simply because we're different?"

"That doesn't seem fair at all," Marnie said. *See? I'm on your side!*

"There is another spell in the works, one that would have the opposite effect," Elaine explained. "One that would open Mystic Springs to the world in a whole new way, one that would allow the magic that encompasses Mystic Springs to spread, and grow, and find."

"Find what?"

It was James who answered, this time. "Springers who have no idea what they are."

Too much information danced in Marnie's head, information that was coming at her too fast. But at the same time, things were falling into place. Bigfoot. Clint. Eve and Ivy. The shadowman. Springers. Clint had used that phrase before, and earlier Elaine had called Marnie a *Non*-Springer.

"Let me help you," Marnie said in what she hoped was a calm voice. "I know this house like the back of my hand. I haven't been here long, but…"

Elaine patted Marnie's hand gently as she rose from her seat. "All right, James," she said with a sigh. "It's likely not here, I agree. I'd like confirmation that the formula has been destroyed, but I might not have that luxury. Burn it all."

Dressed in borrowed clothes that were a bit too large for his trim frame, Lovell devoured two ham and cheese sandwiches and drank a big glass of milk. As he did, Clint explained to the man what he was. A shifter. Bigfoot. Dyn Gwallt.

Lovell was full of questions. "Does the change have anything to do with the moon?"

"No."

"Are all Sasquatches shifters, like us?"

"No. At least, not to my knowledge."

"Why did this happen now?"

That called for a more extensive explanation. Mystic Springs. A genetic component. Springers and Non-Springers. Clint explained as succinctly as he could.

"Did I inherit this from my mother or my father?" Lovell asked.

"I don't know. We'll have to do some research."

Lovell's ancestors might've left Mystic Springs a hundred years ago, or more. Then again, it might've been more like twenty. The surname wasn't a familiar one to Clint, but maybe some of the old timers would recognize it. A trip to the EGG was in order. Those old timers would be a lot of help.

Lovell began to ask questions Clint wasn't ready to answer. It was a lot to take in, in a short period of time, but Clint didn't want to be the one to guide the new Dyn Gwallt along, teach him what to expect, how to handle this new part of himself.

Thankfully, he was saved by his cell phone. He didn't recognize the number, but he answered anyway. A young, shrill voice screamed into the phone. "The librarian is in trouble! Save her!"

CHAPTER 19

Her house was on fire.

Marnie struggled against the scarf that bound her to the chair. It was tied too tightly and cut into her wrists as she wiggled and pulled, but she continued to try. Fire licked the walls, but had not yet reached her. Still, she felt the warmth.

She tried to scream but could not, thanks to her grumpy neighbor who was apparently a witch, or a warlock, or a wizard. A *Springer*, that's what he was.

Moments earlier the old man had flicked his fingers at an outlet in the dining room and had cackled at the resulting spark. Not that anyone would bother to look too closely, but at a quick glance she imagined it would look like an electrical short had started the fire.

Marnie continued to wriggle and pull at the scarf. There. Had it loosened a little? Just a little? Maybe, but not enough. Again, she tried to scream at her neighbor, but he had effectively silenced her.

Elaine tsked at Marnie's struggles, then delved into the pocket of her oversized pink dress to fetch a small vial. Marnie pursed her lips, figuring whatever was in that vial wasn't going to help her escape her burning house. Just the opposite. The old woman caught Marnie's head in a surprisingly effective headlock, pried her lips apart, and placed a single drop of a bitter liquid onto her tongue. The effects were quick. Within two seconds she could no longer struggle, no longer make even the weakest attempt to free herself. Her head fell to the table.

James said, "I guess there's just one place left to check. Where else would Alice have hidden her precious formula, if not here? She did love that library. I can get us in." He looked down at Marnie and grinned, revealing yellowed, crooked teeth. No wonder he rarely smiled! "I've done it before."

Elaine collected her basket and what was left in it, removing the evidence that she'd been here. Marnie watched the two old people who had killed her head for the back door. She didn't think it was her imagination that for a moment, just a moment, James looked like the shadowman she'd seen in her dining room. He'd been searching for the formula then, she knew that now.

He didn't just walk through the kitchen door, he shimmered and a part of his shadowy body passed through the wall. Had he been in her library? Had he left that note, trying to scare her into leaving town so they could search this house top to bottom with no interference? No doubt about it. That creepy grin of his said it all.

Clint had warned her about the senior citizens of Mystic Springs. She just hadn't imagined that a couple of them would murder her.

Witches. Bigfoot. God only knows what else! In normal circumstances she'd love to ponder the possibilities, but at the moment only one possibility was on her mind.

Death. Hers.

She never should've sent Clint away. He was special. The way she felt about him was special. Every moment they'd spent together had been... okay, she'd say it. Magical. Why had she suddenly become cautious now? Why had it seemed like a good idea to take things slow? Talk about bad timing.

She never should've sent that email to Nelson Lovell. For a hundred reasons! Clint was in danger, thanks to her. Bigfoot, with the kind eyes, was in danger. Nelson had been an irritant in what would turn out to be her last days with Clint.

Marnie stared at the window that looked out on her back yard. She loved that yard. It had been hers less than a week, but she loved it.

And the library. She attempted to struggle against her bonds again. Was she able to move just a little bit more? Was she not quite so numb?

The library, *her* library. That's where James and Elaine were headed next, to search for a magical formula. Would they burn it, too? Would they set fire to that wonderful library and all those books? Oh, how it would burn.

Her eyes burned. Her throat felt raw. The smoke was going to get her before the fire, she knew that. They'd find smoke in what was left of her lungs, and some half-assed Springer coroner would rule that her death had been natural. There was nothing natural about this. Was anything natural in Mystic Springs?

She was getting lightheaded from the smoke, maybe from whatever Elaine had forced into her mouth to keep her helpless while her house, and she, burned. Surely that was why she saw something hairy at the window.

Marnie blinked to clear her vision. No, that was not an illusion. It was her Bigfoot, all right.

The back door burst open. The creature that had frightened her as she'd driven into town scooped her up — chair and all — and carried her onto the rear porch and through an opening where the screen door had once been. That door had been ripped from the hinges. Once they were in the yard, cool, smoke-free air hit her face and her lungs. Nothing had ever felt so good. Bigfoot carried her deeper into the back yard, away from the house, away from the fire. Marnie heard sirens in the distance. Whoever was coming would've arrived much too late to save her, but she didn't need firemen. She had him.

Bigfoot knelt down and placed her gently on the grass. He broke the back slats of the wooden chair to free her. She imagined with those hands, untying the knot in the scarf would've been impossible. The scarf fell away, and without hesitation she reached up, her hand instinctively going to his face.

All her life, she'd been a big ol' overthinker. Every decision, every event, every person who'd been a part of that life had been on the receiving end of her analysis. At this moment, she didn't want to think at all.

Bigfoot should not exist. Neither should witches, but she didn't want to think about them right now. The creature — beast, animal, kind being — who held her had saved her. Twice.

"Thank you," she whispered, her voice raspy. "I don't understand any of this. It feels like a dream or a fantasy or a nightmare, but... thank you."

The creature stroked her cheek with one warm, hairy finger. The touch didn't scare her, it was a comfort. He growled, but it wasn't a threatening sound. It was sweet, and oddly familiar, and...

Marnie held her breath as she looked into Bigfoot's amazingly human blue eyes. She knew those eyes. She had looked into them before. And dammit, she knew that growl.

"Clint?"

She never would've thought a creature like this one could have such an expressive face, but there it was, clear for anyone to see. Surprise. Horror. Fear. Did he think she still found him grotesque? That she was horrified by him in any way? Everything in her ached, but she managed a smile as her fingers caressed a very hairy cheek. "Thank you," she whispered.

He gave what could only be called a Bigfoot harrumph, as if he was confused by her response.

"We really need to talk. Later." Marnie jumped up — as best she could, since she still hurt all over and *jumping* wasn't easy — and ran around the house in order to meet the firetruck that was headed her way. The house could not be saved, it was too far gone, but maybe it wasn't too late for the library.

Everything she owned could burn, but that library, *her* library...

Janie Holbrook stood in her front yard, cell phone in hand. She brought a hand to her chest and smiled when she saw Marnie. Marnie waved briefly, but kept her attention on the fire truck. Janie must've called the fire department.

At least *one* of the neighbors didn't want her dead.

The Mystic Springs Fire Department was all volunteer, a fact that was indicated on the side of the red truck that pulled to the curb. That was no surprise, given the size of the town. The four firemen were a mixed bag in age and body type. As they climbed down from the firetruck they looked at Marnie oddly. Two of them visibly hesitated. And then it hit her, why they might look at her this way. She was an outsider, a Non-Springer. She knew what that meant now.

"If one of y'all can wave a hand and put the fire out, don't hesitate on my account. At this point nothing will surprise me." A younger man with very short hair and a distinct Native American appearance ran toward the porch, hands outstretched. She really wanted to watch him work, but at the moment had more important things on her mind. She turned her attention to the oldest man in the crew. He was short, chunky, and had long white hair. She would not be surprised to find out he was an elf, or a troll. Well she would, but that was beside the point. He seemed to be the man in charge.

Marnie called on her most stern librarian voice. "My neighbor James and the psycho bitch who owns the B&B are at the library searching for something. No time to explain what, but if they don't find what they're looking for they're going to burn my library." She lifted her chin and glared at the heavy-set man with the white hair and beard. Yeah, she'd guess troll. She didn't care. "Save it." Her heart skipped a beat. "Please."

The pair who had incapacitated her and attempted to kill her scared the shit out of her. If she had a lick of sense, she'd stay here and let the fire department do their job. Maybe they'd radio their poor excuse for law enforcement for assistance.

But she could not stand here and wait. She'd played it safe all her life, and it was time for that to end.

Marnie kicked off her shoes and ran.

CHAPTER 20

IN THE FADING light of a summer sunset Clint ran toward the library, after hearing Marnie tell Leon about the threat to the library. He loved that library; he'd spent many, many hours in it, as a child and then as an adult. He'd researched each of his books there, had found it a place of peace when his life seemed to be falling apart.

But his love for the place wasn't what spurred him on.

If there was no library they didn't need a librarian, and he wasn't ready to watch Marnie drive away from Mystic Springs.

He had no need to hide himself from the Springers in town; most of them had seen him in his Dyn Gwallt form at least once, but they didn't see him this way often. There was no joy in running down the sidewalk or the asphalt. The forest was his home; the trees were his shelter. He loved the smell of grass and the river and the flowering bushes that created the finest perfumes.

Clint was determined to get to the library before Marnie. She was just going to get herself into more trouble, if she confronted the Springers who had tried to kill her. He cut through a couple of backyards, one well cared for and the other overgrown, and then approached the downtown sidewalk along the south side of the library.

James and Elaine were already inside, looking around, tossing books onto the floor. He heard them, as well as smelled them, long before he pushed his way through the front door. He had to dip down to keep from banging his head into the top of the door frame.

As he pushed his way in, the chime above the door sounded. The gentle noise was almost lost in the sounds of approaching sirens, and the curses of the two elderly Springers who were desperate to find what Alice had hidden.

"There's no time!" Elaine shouted as Clint ran toward her. James, from another aisle, tossed a book aside and cursed aloud. All Clint could do was grunt.

Elaine ran for the exit. James started to follow her, but hesitated. The old man cursed again, and flicked his fingers at a pile of books his partner had rifled through and then carelessly discarded. There was a spark, a flame, and all too quickly a bonfire in the middle of the aisle.

"You should be helping us, not getting in the way," James said, and then he vanished, skirting around the end of one aisle, running as fast as his spindly legs would carry him. For an instant, he was the shadowman, and then he was solid again.

Clint had a choice. Chase James or put out the fire.

The flames grew quickly, flickering higher and higher. The fire truck siren grabbed his attention. It sounded closer and closer. They'd be here soon.

Clint turned and ran, watching as James burst through the front door not far behind Elaine.

James – who was momentarily the shadowman again – exited the smoky library by moving *through* the glass door. Clint was right behind him, but had to wrestle with the door handle for a frustrating moment. His hands were too big, too clumsy. He finally managed to grasp that handle and pull the door open.

Volunteer firemen on the street jumped off the truck. Clint gestured into the library, grunted, and ran after James.

It was no contest. Four long strides, and he had the old man in his grasp. He spun around with James neatly trapped in his arms and saw, down the sidewalk a short way, in front of the antique store, a barefoot Marnie sitting almost calmly on top of a prone Elaine, who still had a bit of fight in her. The seemingly harmless owner of the B&B tried to throw off the woman who was holding her down, but Marnie didn't budge.

All things considered, the librarian looked amazingly at ease.

With James tucked under his arm Clint, still Dyn Gwallt, walked toward Marnie. As he neared, her expression did not change. She did not look afraid of him, or horrified by his appearance. Did she still think him grotesque? It didn't look that way. She remained calm, in spite of all that had happened to her today. The only time she showed a spark of anger was when Travis Benedict ran past her, his focus on the library and the fire truck there.

"I told you someone was out to get me!" she shouted. And then she added, "You'd better save my library!"

Travis ignored her. Clint focused on one thing.

She still called it *her* library.

Defeated, Elaine sighed and rested her cheek on the sidewalk. James didn't have any fight left in him.

Marnie looked up at him. "I suppose we should be ashamed of so violently taking down two old folks, but since they tried to kill me, I have zero remorse."

Clint could only grunt.

"You have some serious explaining to do."

He shrugged.

"But I guess that can wait until these two are locked up and you're..." She waved one hand in a seemingly careless way, "Well, when you're you again. Though I suppose this is you, too. It's my fault. I said I wanted an adventure, and I got one." Her eyes narrowed. "You could've told me."

She looked past his shoulder and grimaced. Clint turned his head and saw Travis walking toward them.

The police chief held up both hands. "The library will be fine. There's minimal damage."

"Thank goodness for that," Marnie said, though her tone was less than friendly. She still hadn't forgiven Travis for dismissing her fears so easily. "I hope you have the good sense to lock these two up," she added.

"You'll have to explain what happened, but I believe we have enough to hold them for now."

"For now?" Marnie stood, and Travis took Elaine Forrester's arm. "They tried to kill me!"

Elaine looked defeated, but made an attempt to argue her case. "We were only doing what's best for Mystic Springs, as we always have," she said. "Are you going to take the word of a stranger over us? A *Non-Springer?*"

"Yeah, I think I will," Travis said as he led Elaine across the street. Clint followed with a silent James in his grasp. Marnie stayed right beside him.

"Maybe he's not a completely horrible law officer," she said.

Clint shrugged and grunted.

Travis saw the two locked up, each in their own small cell. The cells were protected by a spell that muted the powers of those who were detained there. In Mystic Springs, that just made sense. Without that spell, Springers like James could just walk out and disappear.

Once that was done, Clint turned to leave. Marnie stopped him with a sharp command. Then she looked at Travis and asked, "Do you have a change of clothes here? Something Clint can borrow? We need to have a discussion, and I'd like him to be able to speak. It's not a conversation I can have with him naked, and I don't want to wait a minute longer than I have to."

Travis's clothes were too small for Clint, but not by much. They would do for now.

Side by side, they walked down the street. There was no smoke billowing from the library, and the firemen were busy but not frantic. Marnie could see all was well there, or at least as well as it could be, all things considered. People stared, at her and Clint, and she didn't care. She waved a time or two. Some people turned away. Others waved back.

Eve's was too crowded for her purposes, so Marnie walked on by and stepped into Ivy's bakery. It was smaller than Eve's cafe, but was utterly charming. There were a handful of small round tables and white wrought iron chairs with lavender cushions. The case of goodies was well lit; it was a stellar display of a variety of baked goods. Cupcakes, cookies, lemon bars, fancy chocolate what-nots.

At the moment, Marnie didn't care much about any of it. No one else was in the bakery, so she and Clint took a table in the far corner. Ivy appeared from the back, her scowl in place. Marnie looked at her and said, "I'm glad you felt like staying open late today. Can we have the place to ourselves for a few minutes?"

She expected an argument, but didn't get one. Ivy nodded once and returned to the back room.

Marnie gave Clint her full attention. "So, you're Bigfoot."

He just nodded.

"And this whole town is populated with... what, witches, magical beings of all sorts, shifters..."

Again, that nod.

"I asked Travis for clothes for a reason. Speak." She signaled with an impatient circling finger.

First he sighed, then he spoke. "I like you a lot and I want you to stay, but if you need to leave..."

"Who said anything about leaving? Well, okay, I did, more

than once, but now that I understand what's going on everything makes more sense. Not that I think I know everything, but *magical town* is much better than *Twilight Zone* or *I'm losing my mind*." She pursed her lips and frowned. "And I like you, too. A lot." Love? Yes, she was almost positive of it, but was now the time to say the words aloud?

"You'll stay," he said, the words low, soft, as if he didn't believe her.

"For now." Until she knew for sure that she could truly love a man like Clint. Until she knew for sure that this town, and the Springers in it, would accept her.

Like it or not it was on her lips to say *I love you*, or maybe a more hesitant *I think I love you*, but it really was too soon.

Clint parted his lips as if he, too, were thinking of saying something. What? She would never know, because before he could make a sound Felicity skipped into the bakery. With another customer in the place of business, Ivy returned to the counter. Felicity ordered a variety of goodies, and while Ivy boxed them up she walked over to the table where Marnie and Clint were having their momentous, life-altering discussion.

"I hear the library will be back to normal in a few days," Felicity said. "That's good. I need lots of books to get me through the summer."

Marnie nodded.

Clint gave the child a smile. "Thanks for the phone call, kid."

"That's what I'm here for." Felicity leaned in and lowered her voice. "And don't you two worry. It's safe, for now."

Before Marnie could ask what was safe, the young girl was gone. She paid and collected her sweets, which were nicely packed in a lavender box, and was out the door in a matter of seconds.

"What phone call?" she asked.

"Felicity called to let me know you were in trouble." Clint glanced toward the door the little girl had just skipped through.

Oddly enough, Marnie didn't wonder how Felicity had realized she needed help. "Wow. I owe her big time."

"She likes sugar, books, and dogs. Not necessarily in that order."

Marnie smiled. "Then I believe we will be the best of friends." Her smile faded. "The thing that's safe... was she talking about the formula Elaine and James were looking for?"

"I suppose," Clint said, seemingly not at all concerned.

"She could be talking about something else, but what? In a town like this one, anything is possible," Marnie mumbled. "What's going to happen to those two, anyway? How do you punish a couple of... whatever they are?"

"Witches will do," Clint said.

A shiver walked up Marnie's spine. "You can't exactly send them to a state prison, and I can't imagine holding them in the Mystic Springs jail for very long."

"We have ways of handling our own."

"Such as?"

"It doesn't matter..."

"Oh, it does matter. They tried to kill me. They did kill the previous librarian. Yes, they're elderly, but they're also murderers." Scary, cold blooded, and more nightmare-inducing than anything Clint could ever write. "What happens to people like that here?"

Clint took a deep breath and exhaled slowly. "They'll be stripped of their powers and their memories and dropped in the middle of a big city, where they'll be lost in the crowd."

No matter what their crimes were, that seemed cruel. And yet, what they'd done to Alice and had tried to do to her had been cruel, too.

Clint stood, took Marnie's hand, and pulled her to her feet. He wrapped his arms around her. It was a good place to be, and she allowed herself to relax.

"You'll need a place to stay," he said.

"There's the room over the..." she began.

"Stay with me. If you decide you don't like shacking up with Bigfoot, Susan will find you another house. Or you can stay in that room over the library."

She tipped her head back and looked up at Clint. "Why wouldn't I like it?"

"I snore."

"I hog the covers," she countered.

"I'm not particularly pleasant in the morning, before I have my coffee."

"Well, I need a lot of closet..." A terrible thought stopped her in her tracks. "All my clothes, my shoes! I bet it all burned, every single thing. Shit!"

"We'll get you all the new clothes and shoes you want."

Marnie relaxed. Everything she'd lost could be replaced. She was alive; she had Clint. Adventure? There would be adventure around every corner, she imagined.

Why was she overthinking? Why did she hold back? Ordinary rules didn't apply here, in Mystic Springs. "I think I love you."

"I think I love you, too."

With that he kissed her. It was a good kiss, deep and warm; a kiss that connected them on a soul deep level. More than physical, more than arousing.

Ivy snapped at them, breaking the spell. "That's it, get out. Go home. This is a bakery, not a pickup bar. Besides, it's time for me to close up."

Without letting Clint go, Marnie turned and looked at the baker, who in spite of her harsh words wore a half-smile.

"Let me pack you a snack for later," Ivy said, choosing a few goodies at random and placing them in one of her signature boxes.

Marnie placed a hand on her stomach. "Those look so good, but I really can't..."

Ivy caught her eye and smiled. "When I said my baked goods have no calories, I wasn't kidding."

With a grin, Marnie approached the counter and chose a couple of other treats, including the cupcake she'd been craving since coming to town. It was white, with fluffy white icing and two flowers. One pink, one lavender. No calories! This really was a magical town.

"No need to worry about wasting away," Ivy said. "Eve's food has plenty of calories."

Marnie shared that she had never, ever worried about wasting away, and Ivy laughed. She laughed! Maybe there was hope for her yet.

With a lavender box in one hand and Clint's hand in the other, Marnie walked toward the far end of town, heading for home. Could she call Clint's house home? She'd never even seen it, so how could she call it home? And yet, she did. Ahead of her, somewhere in those woods, waited a new beginning.

"You have a lot of explaining to do," Marnie said as they entered the cool shade of the woods.

"I do," Clint agreed.

"I suspect it will take a while for you to bring me up to speed."

He squeezed her hand. "Years."

Years, in this strange place with Clint. The concept didn't alarm her at all. It was right and good. This was her place in the world.

When she'd hoped for an adventure, she'd never expected anything like this.

EPILOGUE

Fall in Mystic Springs brought cooler weather, changing leaves, an obsession with college football, and a wedding.

Marnie and Clint were married beneath a flower bedecked arbor that had been erected at the end of main street for the occasion. Everyone attended, as far as she could tell. Some of the Springers liked her, others didn't. But they all loved a street festival. According to the weather radar it was currently storming in Birmingham and areas south, but there was an odd and convenient clearing over Mystic Springs.

She no longer questioned these oddities.

Her parents might be disappointed when they found out she'd gotten married without them. Most parents would be, but if she was honest with herself she figured hers would be more relieved than anything else. She loved them both, but she'd accepted long ago that she and her parents would never be close. They just weren't built that way.

Clint was her family now.

Her parents might not mind missing this day, but Chelsea would be furious. They'd planned their weddings together, over wine and cheese and sappy movies. Marnie would make it up to her, on short visits to Birmingham with her husband by her side. Once Chelsea met Clint, she'd understand.

From here on out there would be a touch of isolation in Marnie's life, a sense of being separated from the rest of the world. People would get lost; the universe would interfere.

That was all right. She had everything she needed right here.

Oddly enough, Nelson Lovell, who kept talking about moving on but never did, was Clint's best man. He'd changed a lot in the last three months, bulking up, losing the phony accent, and embracing a new love of meat like a truly fallen vegan. He was renting a house on Franklin Road, and while he left town now and then he never stayed away very long. Ivy — who had made a spectacular cake for the occasion — was Marnie's maid of honor. They'd become friends over cupcakes and coffee, Merlot and a secret shared love for the most outrageous reality TV shows.

Felicity was happy to be the flower girl, though she was really too old for the position. Still, everyone smiled as she skipped down the makeshift aisle tossing pink and yellow and white rose petals this way and that. The wind seemed to catch those petals and carry them farther than was natural. They traveled so far they didn't make a path for Marnie. Instead they danced in the air and then fell over the guests like a gentle rain, a kind of blessing, drifting over the crowd and landing on and around the Springers.

Luke Benedict, owner of the local hardware store who always knew what his customers needed, had obtained a certification of some kind online, and it was he who performed the ceremony. Said ceremony was brief and to the point, as both bride and groom desired.

They'd already said everything that needed to be said, in the privacy of their home. All that was left to say was *I do* and *I will*.

The kiss after they were pronounced man and wife was spectacular.

Her name was Marnie Maxwell now, which kind of sounded

like the secret identity of a superhero. Or a super villain. She liked it.

The Milhouse brothers, all five of them, had a band. When Clint had asked the family band to play at the reception Marnie had been skeptical, but the band was surprisingly good. They played country, pop, classic rock, even one classical piece performed entirely on one beat-up guitar.

The bride and groom shared a portion of a dance in the street, and soon others joined in. Marnie realized that she would never be a Springer, that she would forever and always be a Non-Springer.

But she was librarian of the Mystic Springs Public Library, and no one could take that away from her. Thankfully no one seemed inclined to try.

She looked up into her husband's face. "I do love you, you know."

"I know. Love you, too."

He spun her around, and it was wonderful.

Again, she thought about her parents. Maybe they didn't have a great relationship, maybe they wouldn't have come even if they'd been invited, but she should've taken a chance and invited them to be here. She looked around and changed her mind. Still...

"Maybe for Christmas we can go to my dad's house and..."

Clint was shaking his head before she could finish her thought. "You have to be here for Christmas."

She was certain he had his reasons, but still asked, "Why?"

Clint leaned down and whispered in her ear. "In Mystic Springs it always snows on Christmas Eve."

A part of her wanted to ask for more detail, but she'd learned to simply accept. Blind acceptance wasn't always easy for her, but she tried. Besides, snow in Alabama on Christmas Eve? This she had to see.

"Thanksgiving, then. Though my stepmother is a terrible cook."

Clint grunted, as he sometimes did when he was uncertain.

Mayor Frannie Smith weaved her way through the crowd. She wore the same red silk dress and canted tiara she'd worn for the last block party, but this time she wasn't carrying what Marnie now knew was called a funeral cake. Now, *that* was a concept that gave her the shivers.

"I like Mystic Springs," Marnie said. "It's weird, but it's home now, and I love it. There's just one thing it needs."

"What's that?"

"A new mayor. Mayor Maxwell has a nice ring to it."

Clint scoffed. "Forget it. No Non-Springer will ever be elected Mayor. Won't happen."

Marnie smiled as she leaned in closer. "I wasn't talking about me, though I will be an enthusiastic campaign manager."

Before he could protest, she kissed him again.

Marnie was content, settled, whole, for the first time in her life. Maybe Mystic Springs was a weird place, but it was home and always would be. No more running. Everything she wanted and needed was right here.

She had a feeling finding adventure in Mystic Springs would never be a problem.

ABOUT THE AUTHOR

Linda's first book, the historical romance *Guardian Angel*, was released in 1994, and in the years since she's written in several romance sub-genres under several names. In order of appearance, Linda Winstead; Linda Jones; Linda Winstead Jones; Linda Devlin; and Linda Fallon. She's a six time finalist for the RITA Award and a winner (for *Shades of Midnight*) in the paranormal category. She's a New York Times and USA Today bestselling author of more than seventy books. Most recently she's been writing as Linda Jones in a couple of joint projects with Linda Howard, re-releasing some of her backlist in e-book format, and diving into a new paranormal series set in the fictional Alabama town of Mystic Springs.

www.lindawinsteadjones.com
lindawinsteadjonesauthor@gmail.com

Let Down Your Hair

Fantasy/Paranormal

The Sun Witch

The Moon Witch

The Star Witch

Western Historical Romance

Sullivan

Jed

Cash

The Seduction of Roxanne

For more, visit Linda's website!

Made in the USA
Las Vegas, NV
22 January 2021